ATTACKED ON THE TRAIL

The mare seemed familiar enough with the way back to her evening feeding, and some time in the past mile or two Lyle had dropped into a light doze, his upper body swaying and softly bumping with the travel of the unsprung wagon.

He roused at the scuff of boot leather on hard ground.

Lyle lashed out, his fist contacting hard muscle. He heard a grunt of pain and a curse.

The wagon tilted to the other side as a second highwayman climbed on behind Lyle's back while he was trying to fight off the first.

Two of them then. At least.

He felt a blow across his shoulders and upper back. Something hard and slender. A chunk of wood perhaps or an ax handle . . .

Other *Leisure* books by Frank Roderus:

HARLAN
CHARLIE AND THE SIR
JASON EVERS: HIS OWN STORY

PAROLED

Frank Roderus

LEISURE BOOKS NEW YORK CITY

A LEISURE BOOK®

June 2010

Published by

Dorchester Publishing Co., Inc.
200 Madison Avenue
New York, NY 10016

ISBN 10: 0-8439-6273-9
ISBN 13: 978-0-8439-6273-4
E-ISBN: 978-1-4285-0880-4

The name "Leisure Books" and the stylized "L" with design are
trademarks of Dorchester Publishing Co., Inc.

Printed in the United States of America.

10 9 8 7 6 5 4 3 2 1

Visit us online at www.dorchesterpub.com.

PAROLED

CHAPTER ONE

The iron gate closed with a loud crash, a sound long familiar but one he would not miss when . . . if . . . he left this place. He hoped. But then hope was all he had left. Unless he was allowed to leave. If . . .

"In here. You know the way." The voice was crisp but not harsh. There was no need for that and Cranshaw knew it.

"Yes, sir." Lyle Wilson shuffled down the smaller corridor, eyes down and shoulders hunched as if expecting the thud of Cranshaw's baton across his kidneys.

"Stop."

Wilson came to an immediate halt.

"Knock twice."

"Yes, sir." Wilson rapped on the frosted glass panel, then again.

"Come." The voice was faint but clear enough.

"All right. Go ahead."

"Yes, sir." Wilson snatched his cap off and bunched it in his left hand. With his right he twisted the doorknob and pulled. The door swung open and he stepped inside. Cranshaw remained in the corridor.

Wilson stopped a careful two paces in front of the big mahogany desk. He stood stiffly upright, heels together, toes at a forty-five-degree angle. "Inmate Wilson, sir. You asked to see me?"

The warden fiddled with a pipe cleaner, running it in and out of the stem of a briar for some time before he looked up to inspect Wilson. Finally he spoke. "You have twenty months left to go on your sentence."

"Yes, sir."

"I am to inform you that the parole board, in their wisdom and with my recommendation, has seen fit to grant you conditional release."

Wilson felt his knees go weak. Release. The man had said release. Oh, God. He could go home. Sarah. The ranch. Peace at last. He could go home.

The warden continued speaking. Wilson had to concentrate on paying attention to what the man was saying. At the moment though all thought, all feeling, was focused on that single word, *release*. Home. He would be going home.

". . . present yourself to him without delay."

"Excuse me, sir. I . . . I guess I was a little bit overwhelmed there. Present myself to whom?"

"To the county sheriff or his designee. In your case, you being so far from the county seat, I'm told that would be the town marshal of Fox Hill. I understand he is deputized by the sheriff."

"That's the custom, yes, sir."

"You will present yourself to him and let him know where you will be living during the period of your parole. You may leave Alder County only with the permission of either the sheriff or the Fox Hill marshal, and if you should decide to change your residence you will be required to make yourself, and your legal status, known to the chief law-enforcement officer of your new county of residence. You absolutely may not leave the territory, however. Do you fully understand this, Wilson?"

"I do, sir."

"During the period of your parole you may not own a handgun of any sort, although you are permitted to own a hunting rifle or shotgun for the purpose of collecting meat. Do you hunt, Wilson?"

"Yes, sir. Pretty much everybody I know does. Deer, javelina, quail or pigeons. There's good game in the hills around my place."

"You are not to associate with gamblers, prostitutes or other convicted felons, whether parolees like yourself or felons who have completed their sentences. Do you understand this?"

"I'm not sure, sir. Does this mean I can't go into a saloon to have a drink? There might be gamblers or prostitutes in those places, and it's been three and a half years, warden. A man develops something of a thirst in that amount of time."

"Standing at the bar enjoying a drink will not violate your parole. Sitting down at a gaming table would. Or, um, stepping out with a prostitute."

For the first time a slow smile crept over Lyle Wilson's lean, dark face. "I won't be tempted to that, warden. I have a lady back home. I'll be asking her to marry as soon as my parole is completed and I'm really free."

"I'm surprised."

"Why is that, sir? Surprised that a man like me could have a lady friend?" Lyle Wilson knew he was not a particularly handsome man. He was of middling height at five foot nine and weighed a whipcord-tough one forty-five. He had dark hair and clear blue eyes—black Irish, his mother used to say—and in prison had learned to blend into the background, never calling attention to himself if he could help it, never raising his voice, never causing problems. Not, at least, in quite some time.

"No, but I am surprised that you do have one. She hasn't written to you in all the time you've been here. You probably didn't know it, but we log in all communication with the prisoners. Your sheet is empty. I noticed that this morning when I was going through your record."

"Warden, after I got here and—no offense, but after I saw the way things are here—I wasn't sure if I could handle it. Hearing from Sarah would have made it all the worse for me. I wrote to her. Asked her to forget about me and not to write to me while I was here. But I know her. She'll still be there. That's one of the first things I'll want to do when I get home is to call on her and make my intentions known."

"I want to emphasize to you, Wilson, that you must observe all conditions of your parole. If you violate any one of them it could cause your parole to be revoked. If that were to happen, you would not serve the time left between that date and your original release date. Rather, you would have to serve the entire twenty months that now remain on your sentence. Is that clear to you?"

"Yes, sir, it is. But I don't expect to be coming back. I . . . I never should've been here to begin with."

The warden's expression hardened. "Don't start that shit with me, Wilson. We got enough of that from you when you first got here. You caused us all a lot of grief before you finally learned to keep your mouth shut and do as you were told." The warden leaned back in his chair and snorted derisively. "Besides which, there isn't a single guilty man to be found anywhere inside these walls. If you don't believe me, just ask them. They all say they're innocent. They're all liars."

"Yes, sir," Wilson said, his voice soft. Obviously the warden had no idea that in private, among themselves, the inmates tended to brag on their own cleverness in eluding the law as long as they had. They exchanged stories, talked about methods. After his years in prison Lyle Wilson knew how to blow a safe using nitroglycerin or position himself when holding up a stagecoach, or how best to dispose of stolen livestock at auction without the nuisance of trailing them all the way south to the Mexican border. Being in prison had been a wide-ranging education, if not one that he had wanted.

"There is another thing," the warden said. "Don't for one minute think you should look up any of our guards once you get out of here. That would be grounds for immediate revocation of your parole, and believe me, I would see that it happened."

"I don't cause trouble, warden. Not me."

The warden calmed down. "No, that's right. You don't. Not lately. That was in your record too." He picked up a folder from the top of his desk, glanced inside and put it down again.

"Let me tell you how this will work now. For tonight only, you will be moved outside the cellblock. You will be taken to the barber for a haircut, a shave and a bath. Tomorrow morning the civilian clothes you had on when you arrived will be returned to you. You have"—he opened the folder again—"two dollars and twenty-five cents' wages coming to you. You will receive that in the morning before you are released."

There it was again. That beautiful word *released*.

"In addition to earned wages you will receive five dollars specie and a stagecoach pass good for a one-way trip anywhere within the territory. Do you have any questions, Mr. Wilson?"

Mister. God, it had been three and a half years since anyone had called him Mister. "No, sir, I think you've covered everything I can think of."

"Fine. Cranshaw will take you back to your cell now so you can collect any personal items you have there. When you've done that he will take you to a holding cell where you will spend your last night in prison. I trust it will be the last night you spend behind bars ever."

"Thank you, sir. Thank you very much, Warden."

The warden raised his voice and called, "Cranshaw!"

Released. Tomorrow morning. With his own clothing to wear and money in his pocket and . . . and freedom, dammit. Freedom.

Lyle Wilson was atremble with excitement, so much so that he shuffled only a little on the way back to the hated cell.

CHAPTER TWO

A guard named Burnet came to wake him at six. Wilson was already awake, dressed and ready to leave. He had been for more than an hour. Hearing the tumblers turn in the lock and seeing those iron bars swing open for the last time made Wilson almost giddy. He was not sure his legs would hold him when he stood up. They were trembling that much.

He stood. His legs held him just fine, but he was afraid the flock of butterflies in his belly might erupt from the sheer, overwhelming excitement of the moment. Released, the warden had said. Free. He would never have to see the inside of these walls again. Ever.

"You ready, Wilson?" Burnet asked.

He picked up the meager bundle of possessions. Not to include his prison-issue black-and-white-striped clothing. That he would leave behind. He wanted no reminders. "Yes, sir."

Wilson wondered if he was still required to say "sir" to the guards. Not that it made any difference. Not really. The word slipped out now from easy habit.

"Before you leave, you're welcome to have breakfast in the guards' dayroom. It ain't fancy, bacon and fried taters, but you're welcome to it."

"Thanks, but I don't think so." Wilson deliberately omitted the *sir* from his answer. It felt good.

"You might want t' reconsider. It's a three-mile walk to town from here. You're apt t' get hungry."

"Thanks, but all I want just now is to see this place from the other side of the wall."

Burnet nodded. He did not seem at all surprised. "This way then."

There was no ceremony. No good-byes. Burnet led Wilson across the neatly raked gravel yard to the tall main gate. The shotgun-wielding guards on the towers paid no attention. Their gaze was focused beyond the inner wall, where the prisoners exercised and where they passed now and then when moving from building to building.

The tall, always-frowning guard on the main gate—Morrison, Morrisey? Wilson could not recall which—set his shotgun aside and pulled the gate open. It had not been locked. He tugged it open just far enough to allow a man to walk through.

Wilson stopped just short of the gate. He turned to Burnet. "Is this all? I can just . . . leave?"

Burnet nodded.

With a sense of anticipation that suddenly was almost dread, Wilson slipped through the gate and stepped outside. He was leaving behind everything he had known, all the comforting routine, for the past three long years. He felt naked now and vulnerable.

He heard the heavy, metallic clang behind him and turned to see the gate closed. Through it he could see Burnet walking away, back toward his station in the administration building. The gate guard—Morrison, that was it; Wilson remembered it, not that it mattered now; oh, not at all—Morrison reached underneath his dark blue tunic and fetched out a ring of keys. He locked the gate, picked up his shotgun and stepped back.

Wilson turned to face the dry, nearly arid land outside the prison walls. Turned to face much more than that. He was looking now at the future. Home. Hearth. Sarah.

In a rush so great he could have sworn he heard it, Lyle Wilson suddenly felt . . . freedom.

His feet scarcely touched the ground as he shouldered his bundle and began walking toward the town, toward the stagecoach station, that was three miles distant.

Free! Dear God, he was free.

CHAPTER THREE

Wilson's feet hurt. He was not accustomed to walking. Not like this, with dust and rocks and rising heat as the sun came up behind his left shoulder. He was within half a mile of the town—not that it was much of a town actually—when a wagon came into view and turned onto the set of ruts that led to the prison. Wilson obligingly stepped to the side so the wagon could pass.

The wagon, a heavy freight rig pulled by two exceptionally large horses and with a tarpaulin stretched over the bed, came to a stop beside Wilson. "You been out to the prison already this morning?" the driver asked from atop the box.

Wilson nodded.

The driver took a plug of tobacco from his breast pocket and a knife from his belt. He carved off a chew and popped it into his mouth, then offered the plug to Wilson, who shook his head. He would have killed for a pipe and tobacco but never cared to chew. When he tried it before he always ended up swallowing some of the juice and getting sick from it.

"Care to go back out there?" the driver asked.

"Not in a hundred years," Wilson said emphatically.

The driver, a freshly shaved old fellow with graying Burnside whiskers and a slouch hat, laughed. "I didn't mean it that way, son. You're fresh released, are you?"

"Yes, sir."

"Sonny, I live here. We see you fellas come and go all the time. It don't worry me any that you been out there. What I stopped for was to ask you would you like a job."

"I might," Wilson told him. "Depends on what you have in mind."

The man hooked a thumb over his shoulder, toward the bed of his wagon. The team interpreted the movement as a command to start off again. The driver had to haul back on the lines to stop them again. "What I was about to say is that I got near about to a thousand pounds of supplies to deliver and no swamper to help me unload it all. Most of the guards out there are useless when it comes to actual work, so I'd pay you to help me unload. Won't take but a half hour or so, and I'd pay fifty cents."

Wilson shook his head. "Friend, I swore I'd never set foot inside those walls again, so I thank you but . . . no."

"A dollar then?"

"No, sir. It isn't the money and I'd be pleased to help you out if I could, but I don't intend to see the inside of that place, not today and not never."

The driver turned his head politely in the other direction and spat, then turned back to Wilson. "I admire your attitude but I still need the help. How about a dollar and a good meal when we get back to town?"

"Thank you, sir, but I got to refuse."

"All right then. Good luck to you, son."

Wilson touched the brim of his battered old hat and took a deep breath before starting off toward the town again. The brief stop made his feet hurt even more. Or made him think that they did.

* * *

Women. There were two women on the sidewalk. No, three. He spotted another in the other business block, that one just emerging from a store of some sort. Wilson stopped and stared for a moment. He did not mean to be impolite, but . . .

He gave himself a shake. Literally. And took his mind off the two ladies. The two were chattering back and forth. If they even saw Wilson they did not react to him. They went past and turned into the front door of a mercantile. Wilson pushed through the hanging fly beads at the doorway to a place that had a sign overhead that read EATS. After three years of prison grub and three miles of walking on tender feet, he was damned sure ready for some eats.

He dropped his bundle beside one of the stools arranged before a low counter and sat. He concentrated on the menu posted on a chalkboard on the wall in front of him. His mouth began to water.

"What will it be?" the white-aproned cook asked.

"Coffee," Wilson said. "Fried eggs. Ham. And . . . and pie. What kind of pie d'you have?" In the prison there had been no pie or cake provided, and no one sent Wilson any packages containing cookies or candies, like some of the other inmates received from home.

"Rhubarb, raisin or dried apple," the cook said. "How many eggs?"

Lord. How many? He could ask for any number he liked. Incredible. "Three," he said. "Sunny-side up and don't break the yolks. And, um, the apple pie, please." They all sounded good though.

"It will be just a few minutes. You want your coffee while you wait?"

"That would be nice." Maybe when he got home,

he was thinking, he should see if he could buy some chicks. Or even laying-size hens. He could have eggs every day of the week if he had his own birds.

The cook set a mug in front of him and filled it. The aroma was magnificent. They served a hot, dark beverage inside that was supposed to be coffee, but their brew was a poor substitute for the real thing. This was the real thing. Wilson pulled it across the counter so the scent rose to his nostrils and sat for some time just smelling the coffee while the cook got busy with a generous slice of ham and the three eggs that Wilson ordered.

"Any idea when the stagecoach comes through?" Wilson asked.

Without looking around from his stove the cook said, "Official time or when they'll really get here?"

Wilson laughed. "Real then, not official."

"East or west?"

"West, please."

"About eleven, eleven thirty."

Wilson nodded, realized the cook was still looking toward his tasks on top of the stove, and spoke aloud. "Thanks."

When he walked out of the café he felt better than he had in years. Genuinely so.

He tossed his bundle over his shoulder and ambled down the street toward where the cook said he could find the stage stop.

CHAPTER FOUR

Wilson was squeezed into the middle seat between a waddy who smelled of wood smoke and horsehide and a portly drummer who smelled of stale sweat and bay rum. The bay rum struggled to cover the odor of the sweat but it fought a losing battle. Wilson much preferred the clean scents that clung to the cowhand, but after a day and a night in the crowded coach he was more than a little tired of both..

The waddy was slumped in the corner of their bench with his hat pulled low over his eyes, trying to sleep and apparently doing a good job of it. The drummer wanted to talk. Wilson clamped his jaw shut and peered out the window opposite the man. The drummer settled for telling his life story to a Mexican in the seat in front of his. The Mexican smiled and nodded and may not have understood a word of English.

The scenery passing by the coach window had changed from barren desert to lush green as they passed over Angel Divide and started down into the valley of the Fox River. The coach sped up on the downhill slope and the driver had to keep applying his brake to keep them from running up on the hocks of the wheelers. The brake squealed and screeched and sounded wonderful. When they reached the valley floor they pulled into a turnout and stopped to give the team a breather.

"How far to Fox Hill?" the drummer asked loudly enough to make the cowhand stir in his sleep.

The driver seemed not to have heard—or anyway did not respond—but Wilson said, "Five miles." He was smiling so widely that he could scarcely get the words out.

"Is that where you're going, young fellow?"

"Yes, sir. Going home."

"Been away long?"

Wilson shrugged. "Too long." He did not feel inclined to give any more of an explanation than that. It was none of this salesman's business where he had been. Or why. He answered the man, then looked away in the other direction.

Damn but it felt good to be back in the valley. Three and a half years, near about. Yet in a way it seemed like no time had passed at all. Three and a half years. And tonight he could have whatever he pleased for supper. Have a drink if he wanted one. Keep the lamp burning just as long as he wanted. Go to bed when he wished. Or not go to bed at all. If he just felt like standing outside the house, staring up at the stars, why, he could do that. He was free now.

The smile faded. Almost free. He still had twenty months remaining on his sentence. Any infraction of the rules, anything at all, and he would be back inside doing those twenty stinking months.

Up above on the box the driver shook out his lines and popped his whip about the ears of his leaders. The coach lurched into motion again and began to rock and bump and jolt the rest of the way to Fox Hill.

CHAPTER FIVE

Fox Hill did not seem to have changed much while Wilson was away. There were a few more small farms scattered along both sides of the Fox—which was barely large enough for some overly enthusiastic soul to have called it a river—and more people moved along the streets.

The coach rumbled across the bridge that Wilson and several dozen others had built to accommodate their then-new town. The bridge brought back memories of a far happier time. Back then he had known every man in town. And they had been his friends, almost without exception. Or anyway, he thought they were. After the trial he had not been sure about that.

The driver made the turn onto Main and Wilson sat up straighter. He leaned across the drummer to get a better look out the window. There was a new building next to Sam Arnold's granary and livery stable. Sam's place looked the same as he remembered. The new place, squeezed into the space between the stable and Tom Colton's hardware, showed a lawyer's shingle over the sidewalk. GEORGE STANOS, ATTORNEY AT LAW. Wilson did not know him.

There were two other new businesses farther down, one a ladies' ready-to-wear, the other a saloon. Don Faulk's haberdashery was gone, that storefront standing empty. Wilson was surprised how few people he recognized.

The cottonwoods hanging over the banks of the Fox were as he remembered them. He wondered if folks still held picnics there on Sunday afternoons after church services. Those gatherings were pleasant in Wilson's memory. The congregations of both the Protestant and Catholic churches used to eat together at the picnics. He hoped they still did.

Not that he would attend. Not at first, of course. It would be embarrassing. Everyone in town knew about his conviction and prison sentence. Still, if Sarah should want to go, well, he doubted he would be able to resist. He'd already caused her much too much hardship and disappointment. He doubted he would be able to deny her anything now, anything at least that was within his power to give.

Wilson's breathing began to come faster and he felt just a little bit dizzy. This afternoon. This very afternoon he would be able to see Sarah.

He would leave his bundle at the livery, wash up at Sam's pump and head for Sarah's parents' store before he did anything else. Anything at all.

Wilson was grinning so hard his jaw began to ache. He would see Sarah in mere minutes now.

The drummer was saying something in Wilson's right ear, something he paid no attention to, and on his left the cowhand was beginning to stir. Up above the driver hollered "Whoa" to his team and the coach began to slow. It came to a stop in front of the telegraph office.

Wilson's throat was dry with anticipation when the door opened and the driver called, "We'll be here a half hour or so to change the team. Good chance to stretch your legs a mite, and there's a café yonder if you're hungry."

The drummer grunted and wiped sweat from his brow, then climbed awkwardly down from the coach.

Wilson followed. He grabbed his bundle from the boot as soon as a company swamper opened it. He was hungry, but that could wait. First he wanted to see Sarah. That came before anything.

"Say, now, wait your turn," the drummer protested. Wilson ignored him. He headed toward Jim and Harriet Hanson's mercantile at a pace just barely short of a run.

Wilson slowed on the sidewalk, his boot heels ringing hollow on the boards. The hollow beneath the sidewalk, though, was nothing compared with the hollow in his belly.

He stopped in front of the door and stood there for a moment, working up nerve enough to open it and walk through.

Sarah. Sarah would be in there. More than likely behind the counter. She would look like . . . Why the devil was he standing there thinking about her appearance, when he could go inside and see for himself? Wilson silently chided himself.

He opened the door and stepped inside, into the familiar mingling of fragrances from leather and new cloth, neatsfoot oil and packing straw.

Jim Hanson was behind the counter. Harriet was to the right, doing something with a display of small, shiny objects. Sarah was not to be seen. His timing was bad. But then he had not told her he was coming, had not thought to send a wire ahead of the stagecoach.

Jim looked at him and scowled. "Wilson. What're you doing here?" Sarah's father sounded . . . surprised?

Angry? Wilson was not sure. But something was wrong. He was positive about that. Something was definitely wrong with this unenthusiastic welcome from the man he expected to become his father-in-law.

"I, uh . . . excuse me, sir. I've . . . well . . . I've come to tell Sarah that I'm back. They released me on parole. I'm back. Back to stay. I want . . . I want to tell her that."

"My God, man, I thought she would have told you. I thought somebody would have told you."

Wilson's heart sank and his stomach began to turn flip-flops inside his belly.

Sarah! Was she hurt? Was she dead?

"I—I don't know . . . What's wrong, sir?"

Jim Hanson came around from behind the counter and crossed the floor to stand in front of Wilson. He put a comforting hand on Wilson's shoulder. The gesture gave no comfort.

Wilson felt an impulse to turn and run, to get away from here before Hanson could speak. He heard a roaring in his ears and felt a lightness in his head.

"I don't know how to tell you this, Lyle . . . ," Hanson began.

CHAPTER SIX

Wilson was numb, his head full of cotton wool and his heart . . . empty.

Sarah. Jesus!

For three and a half years it was the thought of Sarah, of coming home to her, of marrying her and loving her for the rest of his life . . . it was this that sustained him through those miserable years behind prison walls.

And she . . . Married now, with two small children. One a year and a half, and the other four months old, the grandparents said—Jim apologetically, but Harriet obviously proud of her grandbabies.

Sarah. Married to Bradley Thom, for God's sake. Of all people. Bradley Thom. Thom, whose testimony helped convict Wilson those lousy years ago. Thom, who was big and arrogant and loud. Bradley Thom, who Lyle Wilson loathed. Now Sarah shared Thom's bed and bore his children and carried his name. Of all people!

Wilson stumbled out into the street, nearly caused a wreck from walking in front of a team of dray horses. The teamster's curses reached his ears as if muffled and made no impact there.

He entered the open doorway of the new saloon without conscious thought, the smells of beer and sawdust, old cigars and stale sweat enveloping him, almost comforting. A billiard table stood, unused at the moment, to the right. The bar top was along the wall to the left of the entry. There were two men standing at the far end of the bar. Wilson did not look to see if he knew them. The bartender, a middle-aged man with a neatly trimmed beard, was a stranger to him.

"Yes, sir, what will you have?"

"Whiskey," Wilson said.

"Yes, sir." The man took an already-open bottle from beneath the counter, plucked a small tumbler off the backbar and poured a generous measure. "Fifteen cents," he said when he set the glass in front of Wilson.

"Leave the bottle," Wilson said.

"Two dollars then," the barman said, reaching for a new bottle.

Wilson shook himself. Tried to make the demons inside him go away. This was just another thing that must be borne, that was all. "I'm sorry, I . . . Just the glass. And a beer to chase it."

The bartender nodded, returned the bottle to the backbar and laid down a nickel change from the quarter Wilson put onto the bar. He drew a foaming mug of beer, knocked off most of the head and filled the mug up the rest of the way before setting it beside the glass of whiskey.

Wilson stood for a moment staring at the bar without seeing. The bartender turned and walked down to the other end of the bar to talk with the men standing there.

Wilson suppressed an impulse to scream. Or to cry. Very quietly and with carefully deliberate movements he picked up the whiskey and smelled of it—the scent was bright and strong and pleasant—before downing it in a gulp. He followed the burn of the whiskey with a deep swig of the beer. The two beverages lay warm in his belly, but they did nothing to chase the despair in his heart.

He turned and walked quietly away, leaving the five cents of his change where it lay.

CHAPTER SEVEN

The lobby of the Stockman's Bank of Fox Hill was comfortably cool on the hottest of days, and people tended to speak in hushed tones when they came to conduct their business there. The only other customer when Wilson walked in was a woman—heavyset, barely short of being elderly. Wilson could not remember her name. Not that he needed to. When she concluded her business and turned away from the window she saw Wilson, recognized him and sniffed loudly, her nose headed toward the ceiling and her expression hard as her heart.

Wilson bowed slightly and opened the door for her, giving her no option but to accept the gesture if she wanted to get out of the bank. She did, however, refuse to acknowledge his courtesy.

Wilson chuckled a little as Mrs.—Roberts, that was her name; her husband was the town barber—receded stiffly down the sidewalk, her nose still in the air. Likely she would be pissed off for the rest of the day because of that. It would serve her right.

He crossed the lobby to the teller's cage and nodded. "H'lo, Dave."

"Lyle. Can you wait just a moment, please?"

"Sure." Wilson turned and leaned on the low wall that separated the lobby from the clerical area of the bank. He peered out the front windows toward the traffic on Main Street. A few people walked past. A freight wagon rumbled by in the other direction.

"Lyle."

Wilson turned and saw Cornell Fredericks standing there, looking, as always, completely unlike Lyle's idea of what a bank owner and president should be. Fredericks was no older than Wilson. He was slender and quick of movement. He had come West a few years ago from Maryland with a few dollars in his pockets and a great many plans in his head. He seemed to be making those plans come true.

"It's good to see you, Lyle," he said. His smile seemed genuine.

Wilson nodded. "Cornell," he greeted.

"Has it been five years already? It doesn't seem that long."

"It wasn't that long, Cornell. Parole. I'm free as long as I keep my nose clean."

"I'm glad to hear that, Lyle. Come inside, will you? Come into my office so we can talk in private." He turned his head. "Dave, open the gate for Lyle, would you, please?"

Matthews unlatched the gate and swung it open for Wilson, who followed Fredericks into an office next to the barred cubicle—God, it hurt to look at those steel bars after having been behind prison bars for so long—where the safe and the secure documents were kept.

Fredericks's office was comfortable enough with a settee, upholstered chairs, draperies even though for security purposes there was no window in the room, a handsome desk and paintings on the walls. Wilson did not know much about fine art, but he certainly favored the mountain scenes Fredericks had chosen to display here.

"Sit down, Lyle. Make yourself comfortable. Would you like a brandy?"

Wilson shook his head. "I'm fine, thanks."

"Coffee then? Dave could step next door and bring some coffee."

"Nothing. Really. Thank you."

"Very well then. Business it will be." Fredericks settled down behind his desk and steepled his fingertips beneath his chin. "To answer the obvious questions, Lyle, you do have money in the bank. Not a great deal. A few thousand. I'll calculate the interest and be able to give you an accurate figure in a day or two, but for now please accept that very rough estimate."

"That's all right, Cornell. Right now I just need enough to buy a horse and rigging. I can get that on the way out. But . . . the place?"

Fredericks smiled. "I did just as you asked me to, Lyle. I sold your livestock at auction and deposited that for you. Every year since then I've withdrawn funds from the account and paid the taxes on your behalf. I did pay a commission on the sale of livestock, and the bank has taken fees for the various services rendered while you were away, but I tried to be as careful with your money as I am with my own." The smile appeared again. "More, actually. I don't mind a gamble with my own money but not with that of my depositors. I have a file already complete with the figures from the sale and the commissions and fees paid. You can get that now if you like."

Wilson shook his head. "Another time, Cornell. Right now I'm anxious to get home and see what's left of the old place."

"All I can tell you is that the house is still standing. I rode by there a few months ago. There was a horse in the corral, so someone may be using your place as a line shack. I didn't bother to inquire."

"That's all right. You can't expect a man to bed down on the hard ground and cook over an open fire when he can find a bunk and a stove that aren't being used."

"What else can I tell you, Lyle?"

"Oh, I'm fine, Cornell. Like I said, I just need to get some cash so's I can buy myself some transportation and a mouthful of grub. Then I got to get over to the marshal's office and report in to Marshal Tubb. It's a condition of my parole an' I sure don't want to start off in violation."

"Of course not. But Jim Tubb retired last year."

Wilson grinned. "Did he finally do what he was always threatening to and go sponge off his daughter in California?"

"Almost. He moved out there and bought a little house close to her. He wrote back once and wanted everyone to know that he could see San Francisco Bay from his front porch."

"Good for him," Wilson said. He meant it. Jim Tubb was a good man. Old for the job even when he came here, but a good man. "So who's town marshal now?"

"I, uh . . . He is no friend of yours, I'm afraid. Our marshal now is Brad Thom. I know you and he don't see eye to eye. Especially since the, um, the trial."

Wilson's stomach had almost returned to normal since he sat down and began talking with Cornell Fredericks, but now . . . Bradley Thom, for God's sake. Of all people. Sarah's husband. And the lying son of a bitch whose testimony had put Wilson behind prison walls those long and miserable years ago.

"I guess . . ."

"I'm sorry, Lyle."

"Sure, Cornell," Wilson stood. "Thanks."

Fredericks stood too and followed Wilson out of the office. He paused in the doorway and said to his teller, "Dave, give Lyle whatever he needs. I've authorized his withdrawal."

"Yes, sir."

Fredericks unlocked the gate and let Wilson pass through into the lobby. Then the bank's owner returned to his own office, leaving Wilson standing alone, heartsick all over again.

This was not the homecoming he'd envisioned during those years in prison. None of it.

He sleepwalked over to the teller's window, where Matthews was waiting for him.

CHAPTER EIGHT

The town marshal's office was where it always had been, tacked onto the left side of the large shack that served Fox Hill as a city hall, but there was something different about it now. It took Wilson a moment to realize what the change had been. The marshal's office was larger now. It had expanded to fill the alley that used to run between it and Owen Roberts's barbershop.

Underneath the old and much-weathered streetside sign that informed the passing public that this was the marshal's office, new wording had been added: H. BRADLEY THOM, ESQ.

Esquire? Either Brad had been reading law since Wilson went behind bars or the man was simply putting on airs. Wilson had no trouble deciding which of those positions he suspected. Before . . . before prison . . . Thom had been foreman for the Slash S outfit that claimed a couple hundred square miles lying north of the Fox River. Now the man was town marshal. And "Esq." to boot.

Wilson thought about stepping into Roberts's shop for a shave and a trim before he announced himself to Thom. That would postpone the inevitable but would accomplish nothing. Better, perhaps, to get this over with.

He removed his hat and slapped it on his leg to dislodge some of the dust accumulated inside the coach, cleared his throat and stepped inside the marshal's office.

No one was in there. The discovery was a letdown. He thought he had prepared himself. But not for this.

Still, patience was something he had learned inside a prison cell. He helped himself to a seat on one of the wooden chairs placed against the new wall, placed his hat in his lap and emptied his mind of nearly everything. Everything, perhaps, except for the idea of Sarah sleeping in Brad Thom's bed, cooking the man's meals and bearing his children. But the most galling, the worst to contemplate, was the imagined image of Sarah lying underneath Thom's heavy body.

Wilson tortured himself with thoughts of what the two of them looked like in their coupling. What they sounded like. Thought about the sheen of sweat on their skin and the soft grunting and moist slap of flesh meeting flesh. He disgusted himself with his own imagination, the tricks he had learned in prison turning back on him now to taunt and demoralize. Then, his imagination had been of himself with Sarah. Now . . .

His ugly thoughts were interrupted by the sound of the front door opening and of footsteps.

Wilson jumped up. Without having to think about it he came to the posture that had been demanded of him in prison on those rare occasions when he saw the warden or wanted to speak with one of the guards. His heels were together, toes pointing at a forty-five-degree angle. Hat in hand. Shoulders back. Chin high and eyes straight ahead but unfocused.

"Inmate . . . uh, that is, parolee Wilson reporting as instructed, sir."

"Parolee?"

"Yes, sir." He allowed himself to look at Thom. The man had changed little. But then, to him the time probably seemed short. To Wilson the days and the weeks and the months had dragged endlessly on.

Thom was a large man, half a head taller than Wilson and probably fifty pounds heavier. He was thicker around the waist now than Wilson remembered him to be. He wore a large revolver on his hip and a polished steel badge on his chest. He needed a shave. And a bath. The two stood a pace apart, and Wilson could smell the stale sweat on the bigger man. The thought of Thom lying with Sarah sickened him.

"When did they release you, Wilson?"

"Yesterday, sir."

"On parole, you say. Where are your papers?"

"I . . . they . . . they didn't give me any papers to show you, sir." Wilson dropped his chin and concentrated his attention on the marshal's boots. They were handsome boots, with contrasting stitching and gleaming polish. The leather and the stitching matched his belt and holster.

Thom grunted. "Coming by mail then. That tells me they didn't trust you to deliver them. What do you think of that, Wilson?"

"Whatever you say, sir."

"Look at me."

"Yes, sir." Wilson raised his chin.

"I said look at me, dammit," Thom barked.

"Yes, sir." Wilson allowed his eyes to gain focus.

"You hate my guts, don't you?"

"No, sir." It was not a statement he dared dwell on. "I hate nobody."

"What are the conditions of your parole?"

"I can't own a revolver. Need your permission to leave the county. Have to keep my nose clean. That pretty much covers things."

Thom grunted. "Step out of line, Wilson, and I'll throw your ass back inside. You know that, don't you?"

Wilson continued to stand silently at attention.

"I said you know that, don't you?" Thom growled.

"Yes, sir. I know that," Wilson said softly.

"How long?"

"Sir? How long what?"

"The length of your parole."

"Twenty months, sir. The remainder of my sentence."

The marshal grunted again. "All right then, Wilson. You are free. Conditionally free. As for the future . . . we'll see."

"Yes, sir. Thank you, sir." Wilson turned and shuffled toward the door. It was not until he was outside that it occurred to him how quickly and completely he had reverted to a heavily masked prison demeanor.

Back on the sidewalk he straightened his shoulders and tried to remember to pick up his feet when he walked.

CHAPTER NINE

Wilson's gut grumbled and churned. He had not eaten since the last change of horses on the stagecoach, and the way he saw it, he had gone past hungry a couple hours ago. There was a fine café across the street and he headed toward it.

Leon's Eats was a gathering spot for those who liked to do their gossiping over coffee instead of liquor. It was a place where Wilson had enjoyed many a meal and many an argument.

And he would have friends there.

He paused in the street to let a buggy go past, then stepped up onto the board sidewalk and pushed through the hanging fly beads that covered Leon's open doorway.

As he had expected, the place was busy. There were eight tables in the café plus a counter. Five of the tables were in use, two of them occupied by ladies, and three of the six stools ranged before the counter. Leon was behind the counter. Wilson knew all the men here but two. And all of the women. Sarah, thankfully, was not among those. It had not occurred to him ahead of time to think of what he should do if—when—he came face-to-face with Sarah. It was a relief now to discover she was not here.

Wilson stood in the doorway for a moment. Heads

swiveled in his direction, then turned back and leaned forward.

No one offered a greeting. No one welcomed him home. No one inquired why he was here again when his sentence was not concluded.

Two men, men he had worked beside and shared bread with, men he had thought were friends, actually turned their chairs so that their backs were toward him.

Wilson crossed the room and straddled one of the stools. He knew what he wanted. A mess of Leon's slow-roasted pork with sweet sauce on it, pickled onions and about a peck of Leon's light, fluffy baking-powder biscuits with butter and golden honey. He would think about dessert later.

He sat quietly waiting. Still no one spoke, nor did Leon come to his end of the counter to ask what he wanted. The café proprietor fiddled and fussed around the stove, beneath the counter, sorted utensils out of a basin of freshly washed items. After a bit he picked up the coffeepot and went among the tables pouring for those who might want a refill. When he returned behind the counter he set the pot onto the stove again and disappeared into his back room, where supplies were kept.

Leon did not reappear.

Still no one spoke to Lyle.

After five minutes or so he stood, and as quietly as he had entered, he left the café where his old "friends" were drinking coffee.

CHAPTER TEN

Wilson felt the heat rise in his ears and spread onto his cheeks. He stopped. Took a deep breath and then another. He came away from prison having learned many lessons. One of them was an ability to swallow his emotions. Anger. Or hurt. He felt them. Avoiding that was a lesson he seemed to have missed. But he learned to hold it in and let nothing show. He was reminded of that now. He lowered his chin and dropped his eyes. Took in slow, measured breaths.

The redness faded from his ears and in another few moments he was able to look up again and breathe normally.

The brief incident—or lack of incident—in the café told him much that he had wanted to know.

Yes. His neighbors did indeed think he was a thief. They, or at least many of them, were no longer his friends.

As for others, it remained to be seen whether they thought him innocent or, if guilty, whether they indeed practiced the forgiveness that they preached.

It occurred to him that he had no idea what day of the week this was. He wanted to find out. He wanted to go to church come Sunday morning. That would tell him . . . something. God knew what.

But that would be on a Sunday morning. Right now he was still hungry.

There was another restaurant in Fox Hill, but he did not feel like risking a repetition of that business in Leon's place. He did, however, remember an alternative.

He walked to the end of the block, stepped down off the boards of the sidewalk and turned right into the narrow alley that ran between the building that contained Leon's and one that housed a bootmaker, a tailor and a chemist.

The alley was strewn with trash. It smelled of urine and something he was not sure of. Sulfur, perhaps. He stepped over a broken crate and turned sideways to edge by another. The alley ended at the back of the building block. A screen of brush and cactus ran between the business buildings and the trees that lined the south bank of the Fox River. Wilson turned left, back toward the lone bridge that crossed the Fox, and walked along the back sides of the town's buildings. The little stand was where he remembered—still in business, still infusing the air with the mingled scents of burning charcoal and roasting meat.

"Senor Wilson. Welcome." The old man removed his hat and bobbed his head. His hair and beard were gray and heavy tufts of curly hair blossomed in his ears and out of his nose. He had not shaved in several days. His skin was dark and heavily lined with wrinkles. His teeth, what of them that he had left, were yellowed. He might have been any age from sixty to a hundred. Or he might have been beside this small river, cooking his wares and offering gap-toothed smiles, since shortly after the beginning of time.

"Hello, Pablito. You look well."

"It is good that you are home, senor. If you permit me to say so, you are too thin. You need . . ." Pablo patted his belly and flexed his arms to demonstrate what Wilson needed.

"Will some of your burros take care of that, Pablito?"

"You want me to cook the whole burro for you, Senor Wilson? You want the tail and the ears too?"

Wilson smiled. "Is that really what you put into your burritos, Pablo?"

"Senor! You know me better than this." The old fellow put on a show of great distress at the thought. In truth, Wilson knew no such thing. For all he knew Pablo could indeed be serving roasted burro. Or coyote, bobcat, any damn thing. And yes, with the ears and tails included. But all he said was, "I thought about your burros many times while I was away, Pablito." And that was the truth for damned sure. There probably had not been a week that went by without him thinking of the old man's burritos. And of cold apple cider. Sugar-cured ham. Crisp bacon. Lordy, there were a thousand things he missed. It was no lie to say now that he missed these snacks.

"How many you want, senor?"

"Two. No, three. Make it three."

Pablo nodded and began deftly slicing paper-thin wafers of meat off a completely unidentifiable chunk of meat that sat warming at the side of his grill. He lay three corn tortillas on a smoothed plank and started building the burros from his pots and pokes and bundles of ingredients. He piled meat on. Then spread a generous amount of beans. Added peppers. Poured on a reddish brown sauce that might have contained anything—only Pablo knew for sure—but that tasted wonderfully good. Finally he wrapped each burro with loving care, placed the three onto a flattened corn husk and handed them to Wilson.

"You are just home. If you have no money, pay me later, senor. No, better I think for we to say this is my welcome to you. There is no charge, senor. Not for you."

"You are very kind, Pablo, but I have money. I'll be glad to pay."

"No. Please. Permit me to do this very small thing."

Wilson was touched. Genuinely so. "Thank you, Senor Montez." He bowed, his burritos balanced in one hand. "*Gracias*. Very much *gracias*."

"*De nada*." The old man looked pleased.

That, Wilson thought, damn near made up for the snub he had received in Leon's place.

He carried his hot burritos upstream past the public road and the bridge Wilson had helped build. He found the narrow path that followed the river and took it, stopping once he was inside the thick copse of cottonwoods that grew along the Fox. He found a log to sit on—not the first time he had been on that log, he remembered. The last time he had been with Sarah, and they . . . "Aw, shit!" he grumbled aloud, quickly pushing that thought away.

With a sigh he picked up the first burrito, adjusted the tortilla wrapper in the faint hope that he might keep the juices from dripping out onto his shirt and took a big, wonderfully tasty bite.

Yeah. That was just the way he remembered.

CHAPTER ELEVEN

Wilson felt considerably better when he walked back into town, Pablo's hot and spicy burritos lying warm and comforting in his belly. He headed straight to the livery stable, bypassing the lean-to shack at the front that served Sam Arnold as a business office.

The interior of the barn was shaded and cool—cooler at least than the afternoon heat outside—and smelled of fresh grain and old manure. Both scents were warm and comforting. It had been a long time since Lyle Wilson smelled them. He raised his voice and called out as if to the roof, "Sam. Where the hell are you, Sam?"

Wilson suspected he already knew the answer to that. About this time of day Sam tended to take a pint bottle with him and climb the ladder into the hayloft for a little siesta. He did that most every day, but as far as Wilson knew no one had ever seen Sam drunk. Nor even tipsy, for that matter.

"Wait there. I'll be right down." The answer was slightly muffled. It came from the loft overhead.

Wilson heard some thumping and footsteps; then Sam Arnold's boots appeared at the top of the ladder into the hayloft.

"Who . . . oh, it's you, Lyle. Goodness, son, has it been five years already?" Arnold descended the ladder, one suspender over his shoulder and the other dangling around his scrawny hip. He wore long-unwashed corduroy trousers and a cotton undershirt that once upon a time had been red but now had been washed closer to pink. Sam had been in the territory since the days when there were very few white men around. Back then he managed a stagecoach relay station on the California road. Iron rails and steam engines put Sam's employer out of business. That was when he came to Fox Hill, just beginning to develop as a town, and opened the livery. He had a reputation for a sharp eye but honest dealing.

When he reached the bottom of the ladder, Sam stuck his hand out to shake. "Welcome home, Lyle."

"Thank you, Sam. That means a lot to me." He shrugged. "Not everyone is glad I'm back."

"Not everyone has the sense that God gave a gopher, neither," Arnold dismissed the view of Wilson's detractors. "But seriously. Has it been five years? It don't seem like that long."

"Just over three actually," Wilson told him. "I've been released on parole."

Arnold nodded. "It beats setting in a jail cell, I'd reckon."

"It does for a fact, Sam. The, uh . . . the reason I came by is to buy a rig. A light wagon, maybe, and a horse that can go in harness or under saddle, either one. D'you have anything that might work for me?"

"Mm, I think so." Arnold sucked on his lower lip and took time to pull his other suspender up over his shoulder before he finished his answer. "I got a fine-looking animal. She's been in poles pulling a buggy."

"She?" Lyle interrupted. As a matter of custom mares were seldom used as saddle horses, and men who rode them were subject to teasing.

Arnold nodded. "Ayuh, a mare. But she's built like a stud horse. She's stout. Got a neck on her thick as a bull. She has nice gaits and seems sound enough. I was told she's been under saddle but I don't say that I know it for sure. You're welcome to try her, o' course."

Wilson nodded.

"You wouldn't want the buggy too, would you, Lyle?"

"No, sir. I got no use for a buggy."

"I have a buckboard she'd pull easy enough."

"Let me take a look at both if you don't mind."

"Come along out back then, Lyle. Mind your step." A moment later he pointed and said, "That's her there."

The horse was a bay with a sock on her near forefoot and a narrow white crown on her off hind. She had a white blaze and a neck that was every bit as thick and powerful as Arnold said. And then some. If Wilson had not been told she was a mare he would have sworn she was a stallion. Her coat gleamed with good health. She was in a pen with half a dozen geldings.

Arnold tossed some horse apples at the animals' rumps to get them to move around the pen. The mare moved well.

"You say you've seen her work?"

"Ayuh. But only pulling. I've not seen how she takes to a saddle."

"If you got one I can use, let's find out."

"All right." Arnold tossed a seven- or eight-foot length of old rope to Wilson. "Fetch her out here while I go get a saddle for you."

Lyle ducked between the bars of the fence and walked to the mare. She eyed him with more curiosity than wariness and made no attempt to shy away from him when he draped the rope over her neck, holding it in his fist beneath her jaw. He liked that. Her ears slanted toward him rather than being laid back. Wilson leaned forward and blew softly into the mare's nostrils then pulled her lip down and spit just a little into her mouth so she would forevermore have his scent.

He turned and led the horse back to the gate. By the time he got there he knew he wanted her. Even if she was not broken to saddle he wanted her.

Half an hour later, satisfied that the mare would accept a saddle and rein as well as drive, he told Sam Arnold, "You sold me, Sam. Now let's dicker. I'm wanting the horse and that buckboard, plus her harness. I'm also needing a saddle . . . That one there will do," he said, pointing to the saddle he had been using on the mare, "and the bridle and bit too. Make me a price for the whole package."

Arnold pondered the question for a moment and said, "Let me go set at my desk and calculate."

Wilson said, "Do me gentle, Sam."

Arnold grunted and disappeared into the breezeway of his barn. Lyle Wilson stayed with the horse. He took his time unsaddling and brushing her, then piled the saddle and bridle into the bed of the buckboard that Arnold was selling. Before he had time to finish putting the mare into harness, Sam Arnold was back with a price and a bill of sale.

The price was fair. Money changed hands quickly and Lyle drove away from the livery satisfied with this start on a new life.

CHAPTER TWELVE

The mare drove so nicely that Wilson took her up to the end of Main, turned around and came back just so he could watch her high-stepping trot. On the way back he turned up the short, wide street that had come to be known as Third even though as far as he knew there were no official street designations.

Fox Hill was laid out along the river with one long, virtually unbroken string of south-facing businesses running from the bridge eastward. Across Main from those buildings were others separated into blocks by five intersecting streets that ran north and south. The scattering of buildings south of the Main Street businesses consisted of private dwellings, one small hotel and a whorehouse that was somewhat larger—and considerably nicer—than the hotel. Jim Hanson's general mercantile was on the corner of Main and Third.

Wilson wheeled the mare around to the loading dock on the side of Hanson's building. The news about Hanson's daughter still hurt, but he had done business here for years. And he needed to resupply with food-stuffs and God knew what else if he intended to resume living at the ranch.

"I'm glad you came back, Lyle," Hanson said when Wilson walked in. "I wasn't sure we'd be seeing you again."

Wilson shrugged. For a fleeting moment he questioned whether Hanson cared about Lyle Wilson's feelings . . . or the business he conducted here. That was unkind, he realized. Hanson had given him no reason to think such a thing. "What's done is done, Jim. Decisions were reached that weren't mine to make. I expect I'll learn to get along with them."

"I'm pleased to hear that, Lyle. I'll tell Sarah what you said. I know she will be pleased to hear it." The man smiled and nodded and added, "Now how can I serve you today?"

"Jim, I'm needing some of everything. What's more, I don't really know yet what all I do need. Won't until I get out to the place and see what was sold off in the auction, what might've been stole since I was gone and what might've just rotted and fell away. But for now I know I'll be needing such things as food supplies—a little of almost everything there, I suppose—and ordinary stuff like axle grease and nails. Probably a hammer and saw too. I imagine things like that would've walked away on their own if any were left when Cornell got done with the auction."

"I went to that auction, Lyle. I'd say Cornell sold just about everything he could lay hands on. Got fair value for things too, I'd say. But he didn't leave much behind."

"Just the foods and a few things like that then today, Jim. I'll make a list and bring it in in another day or two."

Hanson nodded and suggested, "I know for a fact your kitchen things went. You'd best take a few plates and cups and like that."

"Throw them in then. A butcher knife too maybe. Forks and spoons. Coffeepot, of course."

"Good enough, Lyle. Let's get busy."

It was almost dark and the wagon was full by the time Wilson rolled away from Hanson's store and started toward his place.

His place. His own place. He almost ached to see it after all this time. He felt a catch in his throat when he thought of it. He was coming home. Alone, which he had not really expected, but . . . home.

CHAPTER THIRTEEN

It was dark by the time he entered the shallow valley where his ranch was located, situated between two of the finger hills that radiated away from the low, rounded peaks and ridges of Jensen's Mountain—named in honor of an early settler in the Fox River valley. Otto Jensen had long since given up on the area and moved on to California but not before he left his name behind.

Lyle Wilson had built near the head of his cut between the foothills. His land ran from the Fox south to Jensen's Mountain. A small but reliable stream flowed from a cirque and ran through his land to join the river east of Fox Hill. His house was modest, built with his own hands using timber dragged down from the mountain behind his little valley.

In the early mornings Wilson liked to carry his first cup of coffee out onto the covered stoop on the north-facing front of the house. He thrilled to the beauty of the land spread out below him, the grass-covered hillsides falling away to the lush bottom of the Fox River valley, the grassy plain lying on either side of the river and the timber that lined the stream.

From his porch he could see neither the roofs nor the lights of Fox Hill, hidden behind the westernmost of the hills that cupped his valley, and that suited him just fine. The town was close enough to provide for his needs but not so close that he had to look at it.

The bay horse labored to pull his purchases up the steady incline from the public road below and twice Wilson stopped, once to give the horse a breather and a second time to wait for moonrise. Only when the land was bathed in the soft, silver light of the moon did he continue on.

The delay was not because he had forgotten the way. Hardly that. Wilson wanted to be able to see his home when finally he approached it.

When it came into view—the house, the barn and scattering of sheds, the corrals and chutes and training pens—he felt a relief so intense his eyes filled with tears.

It was all there. It was all as he remembered.

Wilson had not consciously worried that the buildings would be gone, vandalized or burned, or the materials stolen, but the fear had been there anyway, gnawing away somewhere in the back of his mind.

Now he could see that everything seemed to be there. There was not enough light for him to judge the condition of his holdings. But it was there. That was the important thing. Whatever damage might have occurred while he was in prison, whatever might have been sold off or pilfered since the auction, none of that mattered.

His home remained. He could fix any small problems that might exist.

Wilson paused on the last bit of road below the house and laughed so loudly that the bay's ears flattened and the horse shook its head, sending a comment of displeasure up the driving lines and into Wilson's hands.

"It's all right, girl," Wilson said aloud. "I just remembered something." He laughed again. "I bought damn near one of everything Jim Hanson had in that store. But d'you know what I didn't buy? I forgot to buy any kind of bedding. I came off without blankets nor the makings for a mattress. I don't have nothing like that. But d'you know what? I don't hardly care. I'm home now, girl. We're home, you and me. Now pick it up an' let's us see how things set. Come along now. Hyup."

The iron tires ground noisily over earth and gravel as the wagon rolled the rest of the way into the ranch yard, where Wilson pulled to a halt beside his very own front stoop.

CHAPTER FOURTEEN

Wilson climbed down from the wagon seat. He did not yet know the bay, did not know if he could trust it to stand, so he fumbled on the floor of the wagon for the hitch weight he had placed there and carried it forward. He clipped the lead to a ring on the bay's driving bit and set the weight on the ground, then walked around to the rear of the wagon and let the tailgate down.

Unlike with the bedding, he had not forgotten quite everything of importance when he was doing his shopping. He'd not only bought several lanterns, he had enough foresight to fill one of them with coal oil. Now he took the lantern out and set it on the flat tailgate surface. He pulled a lucifer from his shirt pocket, used one hand to raise the globe on the lantern and snapped the match aflame. He touched fire to the lantern wick, let the globe down and adjusted the wick to give a bright butterfly flame.

He carried the lantern over to the corral so he could satisfy himself that it was sound. Only then did he unhitch the bay and lead it into the corral. He pulled the gate poles back over the entry gap and removed the harness from the horse. The bit and lines he left in place, taking a wrap around the top of a fence post with the lines to keep the horse in place.

Crawling through the corral rails, Wilson fetched a nosebag and grain from the back of the wagon and a currycomb from underneath the seat up front. He poured a gallon of mixed grain into the nosebag and took it and the hard-rubber comb back to the corral.

He affixed the nosebag in place and gave the bay a quick cleaning and rubdown, spending enough time at the chore for the horse to finish most of the grain, then removed both the nosebag and the headstall and again quit the corral.

He carried the harness, headstall, nosebag and currycomb over to the nearest shed. That shed had been a fairly flimsy structure to begin with, but it did not seem to have suffered much while he was away. It was an open-front affair, more a lean-to than a proper shed, good enough to keep rain and the rare snowfall off whatever was stored there.

Wilson delighted in arranging the bay's accoutrements there. He hefted two sacks of grain out of the wagon bed and carried them into the shed too. There used to be an old beer barrel sitting on the right-side floor, but apparently someone had taken that, perhaps at the auction or possibly just helped themselves to it. Whatever the reason, it was no longer there. Wilson would have to get another to replace it. The heavy barrels were perfect for storing small quantities of grain as they would keep rodents at bay.

Only when the horse and its gear were settled did Wilson mount the step onto his front stoop, take a deep breath and push the door aside. His brass hinges were gone, probably pilfered, but come daylight he could find some scraps of leather to serve as hinges. That would do until he could get proper replacements for what was missing.

None of that really mattered though. Such minor annoyances were mere details.

The important thing was that he was home.

Lyle Wilson stood in the filthy, trash-strewn middle of his front room, tipped his head back and howled—literally and loudly—as if bellowing at the moon. His pleasure was simply too great to contain.

CHAPTER FIFTEEN

During his prison in-processing Wilson had been forced to sleep in a spartan holding cell with only a coffin-size steel plate to serve as a bunk, something that could not be burned or befouled no matter what an unhappy inmate might choose to do. He woke those mornings with hips and shoulder blades hurting, the back of his head sore as a boil and joints that were stiff and creaky.

His first morning home he woke on a filthy, cluttered floor that was no more soft or yielding than that prison bunk had been.

But this time he woke up eager and happy and excited about the new morning.

His aches did not matter. They only served to bring him fully awake.

He scrambled to his feet and in the predawn darkness felt his way to the door and out onto his front stoop.

The moon had set but there was enough light from the stars to make out the black-on-gray outlines of his buildings and of the wagon that was parked, still loaded, close in front of the porch.

Wilson waited until his eyes adjusted to the near darkness, then made his way over to the trough that lay half inside the corral and half out, always running full of icy cold water. Long ago he had dug a sump in the streambed well upstream from the house and laid pipe from it to the trough. From there the water spilled out to return to the creek. His gravity-powered water source had never failed and never would as long as there was water in the creek.

Before the trial, back when he expected to marry, Wilson had intended to siphon off some of the flow and pipe it into the house for Sarah's convenience. He already had the spring house built so the cold water could chill milk or meat or other spoilables. He sighed. The piped water indoors would not be necessary now.

He bent down and plunged his head into the water, shivering and blowing when he came up again. But he felt good. Alive. Even . . . happy? Damned close to it anyway.

He shook his head, sending a spray of water toward the bay horse, which had come over to the fence to greet him—or more likely to see what he brought for it to eat. The horse whickered softly and blew a little snot, then dropped its head and drank, its ears working as if they were used to pump the water.

Wilson walked around the trough and leaned on the top fence rail, enjoying the cool, fresh feel of the morning. God, the air tasted so very much better here than it ever had inside prison walls.

He stood there for a time, content, while the sky toward the east began to lighten. When there was sufficient light to make out colors he turned and went back to the wagon. He still had the job of unloading before him and the chore would not do itself. When he was done with that he needed to put the bay in harness again and drive down to Fox Hill for another load, this time hopefully to include those things he had forgotten on his first trip. And before he could do any of that, he needed to sweep the trash out of the house and . . . and . . . He smiled in the near darkness. There were a thousand things yet to do and one by one he would get around to each of them.

CHAPTER SIXTEEN

"Hello, Lyle. I didn't expect to see you back again so soon."

Wilson set the brake and climbed down from the wagon seat. He smiled at the storekeeper and said, "My brain must have been addled yesterday. I forgot almost more than I remembered." He fetched the hitch weight out from under the seat and clipped the lead to the ring on the side of the bay's bit, then lowered the weight to the ground.

"Do you have a list?"

"No, sir. I didn't take time to write one out. Mind if I leave the wagon here for a little while? I want to go find a bite to eat. I'll write out my list while I'm eating."

"You're welcome to do that, Lyle. If your rig is in the way, I'll just move it if that is all right with you."

"Of course it is, Jim." Wilson took a step toward Main, then stopped and turned back. He extended his hand. Hanson, surprised, took it without knowing why. "You've been mighty good to me, Jim. You don't know how much I appreciate that." He smiled. "It seems to be a minority opinion around town these days."

"Don't blame them, Lyle. A jury of your peers convicted you. That leaves a bad taste, and you can't really expect folks to forget that too quick."

"You gave me a welcome, Jim, and I don't believe it

was just so I'd do business with you again. Cornell
Fredericks was pleasant to me too."

Hanson snorted. "Cornell will suck up to anybody
that has more than twenty dollars in his bank. From
what I hear, the bank is shaky. He can't afford to lose
any depositors right now."

"I never suspected," Lyle said.

"The only reason I know—and I know I shouldn't be
talking about this because it touches on somebody
else's private business—is because Dave Matthews is
behind on what he owes me. I've been carrying him
mostly on tick for the better part of a year now and
finally figured out that I might never get paid everything he owes me. Tell you the truth, Lyle, I would've
cut off his credit before now, except he has a family to
feed. Like I said, dammit, I oughtn't to be saying anything about this out of school, so t' speak, but it makes
me mad. All the more so because Cornell drives
around in that fancy roadster of his behind that fancy
black pacing horse, putting on airs and chasing every
skirt in town. Lifting a good many of them too, I think.
Like I said. Makes me mad."

"I'm sorry to hear that, Jim. Maybe you're wrong
about the bank though. I hope so. Wonder if I ought t'
pull my money out and . . . Lordy, I don't know what
I'd do with it if I did take it out. Put it in a sock maybe."
He shrugged. "Not that I should be worrying about
that. There won't be all that much left after I restock
the place. You still have your business accounts with
him?"

"Yes, of course. It's the only bank in town," Hanson
said.

"Exactly." Wilson sighed and touched Hanson on
the arm in a gesture of encouragement, then turned

and headed for the main street. There was another
café in town where he was hoping to find a welcome.
And if he didn't, well, he could always go have another
of Pablo's burritos.

CHAPTER SEVENTEEN

Wilson felt better with a hot meal under his belt despite the stares and the whispers that started when he walked in and continued for most of the time he was there. The questioning looks had not ruined his appetite. Once he was back on the sidewalk he hitched up his britches and frowned.

It was an odd thing, he reflected. During all that time behind prison walls, surrounded by thieves and murderers and scoundrels of all shape and manner, he had not once been bothered by the fact that he had no firearm with which to defend himself should the need arise. But then, in there no one carried a gun. Not even the guards who walked the halls and entered the cells. They carried batons and only batons. There were firearms on top of the walls. All the guards up top carried shotguns and in two of the towers, the ones at cattycorner ends of the compound, there were gleaming brass Gatling guns. Wilson had never seen a Gatling in action but he had heard enough about them to know that he did not want to. Not when he might be standing in front of one. The inmates all had a healthy respect for the Gatling guns.

Here on the main street of Fox Hill, in broad daylight in a town filled with women and children, Lyle Wilson felt an emptiness on his right hip. Nearly all the adult men in town wore handguns on their belts as a matter of habit, if not of need.

There probably—no, certainly—was no real need for that. Not now. There was no danger now from marauding Indians or robber gangs from south of the border. There might have been once, but those days were long gone. Now people settled their disputes in courts of law.

Even so, Wilson was mindful of the parole restriction that kept him from owning, much less wearing, any sort of handgun.

He snapped his fingers. A shotgun. He forgot to buy a shotgun and shells yesterday. He should have put a shotgun on his list. If he had a list. He had forgotten to write that out while he was at lunch too. Sometimes he thought his brain was turning to mush.

Wilson's lip twisted with distaste at the thought of mush. Cornmeal mush had been one of the staple foods served inside. Except *served* was not a proper word for the distribution. The stuff, heavy and sticky and bland, was ladled out a quart at a time onto steel plates, without even any salt to give it flavor. If Wilson never ate mush again in this lifetime it would be too soon.

Anyway, he needed to buy a shotgun. A good shotgun and some buckshot would do him to hunt deer or javelina. Small shot for birds and rabbits, heavy shot for larger game, and he would not have to waste money on a rifle. Without a rifle he could not reasonably expect to hunt antelope, but that was all right. Antelope was not one of his favorite meats anyway. He much preferred venison.

Wilson was deep in thought, trying to work up a mental list of the things he should buy this time, when he nearly bumped into a lady pushing a perambulator.

"Pardon me, ma'am." He snatched his hat off and stepped quickly to the edge of the sidewalk. "Oh . . . I . . . didn't see who it was. Right off. Uh . . . well . . . I mean . . ."

"There's no need to apologize, Lyle. Daddy told me you were out. Are you well? Did they treat you all right?"

"Yes, I'm . . . fine." He felt awkward and foolish. It was inevitable that he would encounter Sarah Hanson—Sarah Thom—sooner or later. Later would have been preferable. He just was not ready to see his one-time fiancée. Not yet.

Now she obviously had stopped by the store to see her parents and was on her way back into town. To her home perhaps, wherever that might be. He had not asked. Or to shop or visit or . . . or to drop by the marshal's office to see her husband.

How strange was that thought. To see her husband.

Wilson looked down at the two children, one barely big enough to be walking and the other little more than a tightly wrapped bundle of pink cheeks and bald head.

"They, uh, they're mighty pretty," he managed, pointing vaguely in the direction of the children who lay in the white-tasseled navy blue perambulator. The older of the two looked at him with huge, dark eyes. "What are they?"

Sarah smiled proudly. She came around to the side of the basket and bent over her wee ones. She touched the curly hair on the older one and said, "They're both boys. This one is Bradley Junior. This one"—she touched the naked head of the infant—"is Bryan."

"They're handsome boys, Sarah. I'm sure you are proud of them."

"I am. Very proud." She straightened upright, her chin high. "Very proud."

"You . . . I'm glad you didn't write," Wilson said.

"You told me not to."

"I did. Yes."

"Are you really all right, Lyle?"

"Fine, thanks." All of a sudden he was not so sure about that, but it was what he had to say to a question like that. "And you? Are you well?"

"Yes. Of course. How could I be anything but fine? My husband is greatly respected. We have a fine home. Fine sons. Yes, Lyle, I'm well."

"I'm glad to know that, Sarah. I . . . I best get along. I got lots to do. Getting the place back in shape and everything. You understand."

"Yes, of course." Sarah took hold of the handle of her perambulator and the wheels of the child carrier rumbled on down the sidewalk.

Wilson stood there for a moment, staring toward a blank wall that had the remnants of some old handbills pasted on it. He fought back an impulse to turn and watch Sarah's receding back. Receding backside was more like it. He had always admired the shape of her. Then. He could not do that now. Now she was a respectable married woman with two small children and a husband.

Not only a husband, Wilson reminded himself, but this particular husband could terminate his parole if he stepped over the line.

Wilson forced himself to display a calm that he did not necessarily feel, an ability that he had found and had nurtured during his years in prison. His expression showed nothing of what he was feeling.

After a few moments, Wilson tugged his hat back on, took a deep breath and resumed his brisk walk toward Jim Hanson's store.

CHAPTER EIGHTEEN

Wilson set the chair onto its legs and gave it a wiggle. The newly replaced leg was ugly, being a piece cut from a discarded board and not a nicely turned cylinder like the other three legs, but the thing seemed sturdy enough. He sat on the chair, rather gingerly at first, then smiled when it held his weight. He had already fashioned a table of sorts out of scraps of wood scrounged from the trash pile, so now he had a table and chairs. A cot would be next in the furniture department but that could wait. Now that his mattress ticking was filled with dried grasses he would be comfortable enough on the floor.

He glanced toward the lightweight sheepherder's stove he had bought in town to replace the cast-iron stove that used to sit in that corner. Wisps of steam were rising from the bucket of water there.

"Good," he grunted. "'Bout damn time." Wilson crossed the room to the stove and peered into the half-full bucket. He was tempted to poke a finger into the water to check the temperature but resisted the impulse. The water was not boiling but it was plain enough that it was hot now.

He took a block of Fels soap down from the shelf where he had put it, opened his pocket knife and began slicing curls of the hard yellow soap into the near-boiling water. The familiar odor of naptha quickly filled the room. When he decided there was enough soap in the water he replaced the block onto the shelf and picked up a stick, using that to stir the soap chips so they would dissolve sooner. Once the solution was a cloudy white with no visible pieces of soap, Wilson laid the stick back into the wood box and glanced around to make sure nothing important was down where it could get wet. Then he picked up the bucket by the bail and, using a now-empty piece of burlap sacking to hold onto the hot bottom, tilted the pail and splashed hot, soapy water onto the floor. He kept that up until the floor was fairly thoroughly covered.

He did not own a mop but for this a broom would surely do. He began scrubbing the floor with the stinking naptha soap, starting at the back wall and sweeping the dirty water forward as he scrubbed.

He was about halfway toward the front door when he heard hoofbeats outside and a man's voice call out, "Mr. Wilson. Hello in the house. Are you in there, Mr. Wilson? May I step down for a moment?"

"Well, shit," Wilson mumbled under his breath. Whoever this was—probably some sort of damned salesman—the scrub water would be cold by the time he could come back inside, and then it would not do as good a job as he wanted. He considered just going on with what he was doing, and never mind the uninvited and indeed unwanted visitor out there.

"Mr. Wilson. Please?"

Grumbling still, Wilson set his broom aside and walked out onto the stoop.

CHAPTER NINETEEN

The man sat on the seat of a lightweight doctor's buggy that was stopped close in front of Wilson's front stoop. The rig was pulled by a sleek, powerfully muscled black horse. The driver, on the other hand, did not have a look of power about him. If anything, he seemed puny, like someone who had just risen from a sickbed.

He was thin to the point of being unhealthy. He was probably still in his twenties and was pale beneath a shock of unruly reddish blond hair. He had blue eyes, a long nose and freckles. A very prominent Adam's apple bobbed up and down when he swallowed. He wore a boiled shirt with a celluloid batwing collar attached, a rather sloppily tied necktie and black broadcloth trousers but no coat. Wilson could not see either a badge or a gun.

The man smiled. "May I step down?"

Wilson shrugged. "I suppose so. I'll listen to your pitch. Might even buy something off you, but that will depend on what you're selling."

The visitor laughed and climbed down from the seat of his buggy. He looked around for a hitching post and, failing to find one, took a weight and lead from the floor of the rig and saw to the horse.

"You're welcome to water him in the trough there," Wilson offered.

"Thank you, but I already let him drink from the creek yonder."

"I can't invite you in. Got no furniture yet. Not enough for company anyway. You, uh, wouldn't happen to be selling furniture, would you?"

"Oh, I'm selling something much more valuable than furniture," the visitor said with a smile.

"More valuable than . . . Mister, I don't have a lot of money. I can't afford extravagances. If somebody told you otherwise, they told you wrong."

The smile flashed again, wider than ever this time. "Friend, what I'm selling won't cost you a cent but it will pay you huge dividends." The man turned around and fetched a book from the seat of the buggy. The book was large and leather bound. It was worn and scuffed from much use. The page edges once were gilded but most of the color had been worn away with age and much handling.

"You're a preacher," Wilson said.

"More than that, I'm a pastor," the man told him. "I'm Evan Moore. I'm pastor of the Fox Hill Methodist Church."

"What happened to the Reverend Talbot, Reverend Moore?"

"First, unless you have some odd reason to revere me, you needn't call me Reverend. Pastor, if you insist on a title. Or Mister works just as well. What I prefer is to be called Evan. As for Reverend Talbot, we Methodists tend to move pastors around every year or two. It keeps people from becoming entrenched and mentally lazy. Keeps things fresh, you see."

"I'd heard that, I suppose. Just didn't think much about it either way."

"You are not a churchgoing man then," Moore suggested.

"No, sir."

"Perhaps you should be. It might be a point in your favor with the people at the Bureau of Prisons. Should the need arise, that is."

"Are you in need of parishioners, Evan?"

"Me? No. But I think you could use a few sermons, Lyle. Do you mind if I call you Lyle?"

"No, I don't mind."

"Good, because it's a name that is on the tip of many tongues down in town right now." He smiled again. "If nothing else, Lyle, you've provided hours and hours of gossip to the folks down there."

"I kinda suspected that much. Look, can I get you something? I . . . Damn. Now that I think about it, there isn't much I could offer. Water. That's about it."

"A drink of water would be splendid. Walk with me, Lyle?"

The two ambled over to the corral, where the standpipe faithfully ran icy-cold creek water into the trough. When he stood beside the man, Wilson found himself half a head taller than Evan Moore, and Wilson was himself not particularly tall.

Moore cupped his hand under the outflow and took his time drinking from it, then splashed some of the cold water onto his face and the back of his neck before he straightened. "That's invigorating," he said. They turned and started slowly back toward Wilson's cabin. "I hope you know you will be welcome in services any Sunday. Every Sunday. But you might want to make it a point to be there tomorrow." Moore chuckled. "After all, you will be the subject of my sermon. Which is one of the things that brought me out here today. That and to meet you and to let you know that I would be pleased to see you there any time."

Wilson grunted. "Preaching on the evils of stealing, are you?"

"On the benefit of forgiveness actually," the preacher said.

"Serious?"

"Mm, yes."

"I'll be damned," Wilson said.

Moore laughed. "Oh, I hope not. Not being damned is the whole idea, isn't it?"

He reached his rig, returned the hitch weight to the buggy floor and his Bible to the seat and climbed into the buggy. Moore reached down and offered his hand to shake, which Wilson did.

Wilson was expecting the preacher to pray over him then or offer words of benediction or some damn thing, but he didn't. He just said, "I'm pleased to have met you, Lyle. I hope you will come down tomorrow. Services start around eleven or so." Then he unwrapped his reins from the empty whip socket, clucked to the black and wheeled on down the path toward the road to Fox Hill.

Wilson watched him out of sight, not entirely sure how he should take the young preacher. The little fellow was not what he normally thought a preacher would be but . . . he kind of liked him. Maybe he would go down to town tomorrow. Maybe.

CHAPTER TWENTY

"Guess who we just seen coming inta town? Go ahead. Guess. You ain't gonna guess it in a hunnerd years."

Bradley Thom looked up from using a dandy brush to rub bootblack into his Sunday shoes. "What are you boys doing here so bright and early?"

"Your missus said you was around back here. You don't mind?"

"No, I don't mind you coming by." Thom took a few more swipes at the toes, then set the shoes down on the boards of his small back porch. He slipped his feet into them, the right first, then the left. He crossed his left leg over his right knee and leaned forward to tug the laces snug and tie that shoe. He straightened with a belch and a sigh, then repeated the process with the other leg.

"You ain't guessed who we seen. Hah! Knowed you couldn't do it."

"Lyle Wilson," Thom said without looking up from finishing with the right shoe.

His visitors' faces fell. "How . . . ?"

The Fox Hill town marshal laughed and stood upright, looking down at Willy Bannerman and Tom Hart, who stood beside the porch peering up at him. "I'm the marshal, remember? I'm the one Wilson had to report to when he got released on parole."

"Oh. I, uh, never thought o' that."

"I also got a report on him from the prison warden. Lyle Wilson learned to be a good boy while he was inside. He learned to shut his mouth and do what he's told. And he won't want to go back there, which he damn sure will do if I find him in violation of any of the terms of his parole. I'm not expecting any trouble out of him. You shouldn't either."

"Yeah, but . . . we testified. Right there in open court, with him setting not fifteen feet away. It was all written down. He knows what we said about him."

Thom glanced around to make sure Sarah was not lurking anywhere nearby, then turned back to his visitors. "If Wilson says anything to either one of you, I'll put him right back in there, and he knows it. You don't have anything to worry about."

"What if he figures out that you—"

"I didn't do nothing. You got that? Nothing. And don't you be suggesting otherwise. Even if somebody proves Wilson was innocent, you're both in the clear. You just say you made an honest mistake and let it go at that. Understand?"

"If you say so."

"Aye, I say so. Now get out of here before someone sees you hanging around." Thom winked at them. "I have to protect my reputation, you know."

All three men laughed at that.

CHAPTER TWENTY-ONE

All in all, Wilson thought, the morning had not gone too badly. He knew probably three-quarters of the congregation, and none of them snubbed him. No one cozied up to him either, but they were neutral, and that was the best that he might have hoped for.

The little preacher, Evan Moore, shook Wilson's hand just like he did all the others as folks filed past him in the open doorway at the conclusion of the services. Wilson wondered as he made his way back out into the midday sunshine whether any of them made a connection between his appearance and the message of forgiveness they just heard inside. Probably not, Wilson conceded. Most of them likely had no idea where he had spent the last few years. Or why.

Some did, of course. And by day's end the rest of the folks would know about it too. The spread of information that there was a convicted sinner amongst them would begin immediately as people brought food baskets out of their buggies and headed for the shaded picnic grounds down by the river. The congregation would eat together. And talk together. And those few who did not already know very soon would. Wilson wondered if he would be welcome here next Sunday. He really was not sure that he should come down to town again and find out. Better, perhaps, to stay at home.

In the meantime, he was hungry. He had not thought to bring anything to eat after the service and now his stomach was growling.

"Join us," a tall, smiling gentleman said, a handsome wife and two young sons beside him.

"We have plenty enough to share," the lady said.

"Oh, I . . . I thank you. You're very kind. But I'd . . . better not."

"We know who you are," the man offered. "You needn't worry about those who spread gossip."

Wilson was taken aback. They knew. They invited him anyway. He felt deeply touched by their offer. But not so much so that he wanted to subject himself to the scrutiny—and the unspoken judgment—of others at the after-church picnic. "Thank you," he repeated, meaning it sincerely. "Thank you, but . . . not today."

"Next Sunday perhaps," the gentleman said. He turned and led his family around toward the back of the white-painted church building. As they went the mother said something to her sons, and the boys both bolted toward the lot where the buggies were parked. Going to fetch their family's basket, Wilson assumed.

Wilson's stomach grumbled anew at the thought of picnic fare. Fried chicken and sour pickles and hard, crusty breads served with soft cheese. He really should have taken time for breakfast earlier. But then he would have been late for Reverend Moore's church service, and he was sure he would not have had the courage to walk in during the middle of things.

Still, he needed something to eat, and pretty much all the businesses in town would be closed. Everything, that is, except the saloons and—if he was in luck—the cafés.

He untied the mare from the post where he had left

her, took hold of her bit and backed her away from the crush of other parked rigs and climbed onto the seat of his wagon.

Main Street looked like Fox Hill had suddenly become a ghost town. Practically everyone in town was either at one of the churches, was propping up a bar in one of the saloons or was still sleeping off last night's exertions.

A whore in a bright red Chinese-patterned kimono came out onto a balcony over the bakery, paused and turned her head to listen to someone inside the building and quickly disappeared again.

A pair of cats got into a screeching, hissing fight in the alley beside the millinery.

A handful of pigeons fluttered down to pick at the horse droppings scattered in the street.

Sunday.

"Dammit," Wilson muttered to himself. The one café where he seemed to be welcome nowadays was closed. The other . . . Not that it mattered, but it was closed too.

Pablo Montez, thank goodness, should be open for business beside the river farther upstream. Pablo would want to get as much of the after-services trade as he could once the Catholic mass let out.

Wilson clucked to the mare and put her into a trot, heading toward Pablo's little burrito stand.

CHAPTER TWENTY-TWO

"This is mighty good, Pablo. *Gracias.*" Wilson felt better with three of the spicy, tortilla-wrapped burritos under his belt. "Thank you very much."

"Another, senor?"

Wilson shook his head and rubbed his belly. "No more today. I'm full as a tick on a dog's ear. They're good though. Maybe next week."

"Next week"—Montez shrugged—"I maybe will not be here. No more little burros, I think."

"Why is that, Pablo? Will you be taking a vacation? Taking some time off?" His mare stamped her right forefoot impatiently. Wilson guessed she was smelling the horses in Sam Arnold's feedlot. The livery was not far from the bridge where Pablo always set up and the breeze was from that direction.

"Time off? No, senor. I will have no meat to sell, I think. Not the good meat like this."

Wilson raised an eyebrow, encouraging Montez to go on.

"No more cabrito," the old man said.

"Is that what this is? I didn't know."

"*Si.* Goat. *Cabra.* But young. Very tender. Very good to taste. Cabrito."

"Kid," Wilson said.

"*Que?*"

"Young goat we call kid. The meat from kids we call cabrito. I suppose we got that from you, since it's the same in both languages. But the young animal we call a kid. Why won't there be any more cabrito, Pablo? Won't other meats do as well? I don't know . . . beef, lamb, something like that?"

"Yes, other meats would make a burro. Even the meat of a burro could be used to make a burro. But it would not be the same. Only meat from the cabrito makes the very best burro. All the others . . . not so good."

"So anyway, why won't you have any more cabrito, Pablo?"

"The, uh, kid . . . Is that how you say it?"

Wilson nodded.

"The kid I buy from my fren Luis Santiago. Luis, he work for Senor Donovan. Luis tells me Senor Donovan will sell his herd. No more *cabra*. No more cabrito. No more job for Luis."

"That's a shame, Pablo. I'm sorry about your friend."

Montez shrugged. "It is life. It is hard. But what is a poor man to do, eh?" He smiled. "One more burro, senor? While I still have the cabrito?"

Wilson thought his belly might bust when he finally crawled back onto the seat of his wagon and headed for home.

CHAPTER TWENTY-THREE

On the way out of town Wilson saw the two saddle tramps whose testimony at his trial had served to put him behind bars. The two were lurking on the steps outside of Jolly's Saloon. He had no trouble recognizing the men. He had thought of them often over the past few years.

Bannerman was the shorter, thicker-bodied one of the pair. He looked like he had not washed since the last time Wilson saw him. And that was on the witness stand. For all Wilson knew, the bastard might not have changed his clothes either. Tom Hart was a little taller, a little lighter built. Bannerman had a beard, while Hart was more or less clean-shaven. At the moment Hart looked like he could use another trip to the barber's for a shave and a trim.

For a few seconds there, Bannerman's first name slipped Wilson's mind—just a month ago he would not have thought that possible—then he snapped his fingers and grunted. Willy. That was the SOB's name. Willy Bannerman, may he rot in hell for the lies he told under oath. Three years of his life those lies had cost Lyle Wilson. Three miserable years.

He did not want to make it five.

Wilson averted his eyes and turned his head away when his wagon rolled past the two liars.

Once clear of them he gave a little shake to the lines and picked the mare up into a trot.

When he passed the picnic grounds, the folks from church were still there, many of them anyway. He could see the grown-ups sitting on the log benches under the trees, surrounded by baskets of food. More than a few jars of beer had appeared as if out of nowhere as well.

On a soft green flat closer to the road, a gaggle of children ran and rolled in the grass as they pursued some game or other. Their voices were high-pitched and clear.

Wilson turned his head from the children too.

It used to be that he enjoyed the sight of children playing. But then he used to look forward to having some of his own.

Now . . . now he acknowledged that he very likely would live out his days childless and a bachelor.

That was not an attractive prospect. Certainly it was a thought he did not want to dwell upon.

"Hiyyup. Git up there," he chirped to the mare. He gave another shake to the lines and she extended her trot.

Of a sudden he was anxious to get home. He had work to do, dammit.

CHAPTER TWENTY-FOUR

Wilson stopped what he had been doing and straightened upright, sweat glistening on his chest and fresh sawdust mixing into it to form a sort of gritty mud on his flesh. He carefully lifted the blade of the big Swedish bow saw out of the cut he had been making and set the saw frame aside. He picked up a rag and used it to wipe his face and mop some of the sweat off his neck and torso. He twisted the rag into a tight knot to squeeze some of the moisture from it, then spread the wet cloth wide and hung it onto the far upright of his sawbuck. Then he stood, chest heaving from the continued exertion, and waited for the riders to reach him.

That was one of the good things about his place. If anyone approached up the road he could see them a good half mile away. Should anyone want to surprise him they could pop up over one of the two ridges that flanked his little fold in the mountain. But that was unlikely. It was much more work than just coming up the road from the river valley below.

There were four, he saw. As they came near he recognized Bradley Thom in the lead along with Ned Weathers and two men he did not recognize. Weathers, he recalled, was a crony of Marshal Thom. The two used to ride together on the Angel spread and maybe some others as well. Before he went looking for respectability, Thom had ridden for several different outfits. Ned Weathers had too, Wilson remembered.

The four horses came in at a trot and pulled to a halt not at the water trough but close to the sawbuck where Lyle Wilson stood.

"H'lo," Wilson said, keeping his eyes down and his voice neutral. He reached for his shirt and drew it on but did not bother with the buttons. The cloth of the shirt clung to the moisture that remained on his skin. It felt uncomfortable and now there would be bits of sawdust clinging to the inside of the shirt. He would have to launder the shirt to get rid of them and he needed to bathe himself if he wanted to keep from carrying the sawdust into his bed tonight as well.

None of the riders behind Thom said anything and Thom himself took his time about speaking. Enjoying himself, Wilson guessed. Finally the marshal spoke.

"Where were you last night, Wilson?" Thom's voice was harsh, its tone accusing as much as it was demanding. His horse, a pale sorrel with too thin a neck for the size of its jaw, began to fidget beneath him. Thom snatched at the bit to bring it back into line and cursed under his breath.

Wilson kept his eyes down, but he could not help noticing that the other riders drifted their horses wide apart so that all four of them were looking down on him from an arc.

"I asked you a question, mister," Thom barked. "Where!"

"Here. Home. Where I always am," Wilson said.

"Here what?"

"Here, sir!" Wilson said quickly. Having to say that made his skin crawl, but the lessons learned behind those stone walls were lessons deeply ingrained.

"Got anybody who can confirm that?" Thom demanded.

"No, sir. I'm . . . I live alone. I didn't have any visitors. Haven't spoke to another soul since last Sunday, sir."

Thom turned his head. "Ives. Lewis. Is this him, d'you reckon?"

"No, Marshal. That fellow was bigger than this 'un. Don't you think so, Billy?"

"A lot bigger," said the other of the strangers Wilson did not know. "Shorter hair too, that one did."

"All right then," Thom growled. "They say they don't think it was you. That ain't proof, mind. That's opinion. Do I find reason to change my mind about you, I can still come out here and arrest you. Drag your sorry ass right back into a cell where you belong."

"Yes, sir. I understand, sir," Wilson said meekly.

"Come on, boys. We'll look somewheres else." Thom hauled the sorrel's head around and gigged the animal with his spurs. The other three followed with more deliberation.

"You're welcome to water if you like," Wilson said to their backs, looking up for the first time in a while. "You and your horses too."

One of the men he did not know, either Ives or Lewis he would be, turned in his saddle and gave Wilson a friendly enough smile. "We better catch up with the marshal, but I thank you." The smile grew. "Next time, okay?"

Wilson nodded, and the three riders spurred ahead to catch up with Bradley Thom, who was already a good seventy-five yards ahead of them.

Lyle Wilson took himself up on his own good offer. He walked over to the water trough and helped himself to a dipper of it. It did taste good going down.

CHAPTER TWENTY-FIVE

Wilson set the sack of cornmeal onto the counter in Jim Hanson's mercantile. "Dammit, Jim," he muttered, "you know what I think I resent even more than being rousted like that? It's not being able to do anything about it. Nothing. Nothing at all."

The older man grunted noncommittally and busied himself with transferring Wilson's cornmeal onto his hanging scale. He kept one hand on the scale to stop the cornmeal from swaying. Then, once the big steel scoop was steady, he took the hand away. "Nine pounds five ounces," he said.

Wilson went on as if he had not heard. And in truth he had heard, but the words had not registered. Wilson's thoughts were focused on the incident in his yard the previous afternoon. "You see, the thing I really hate about this is that he can come at me any time he wants and do it with the weight of the law behind him. And there's no one, not a single soul, that I can turn to t' plead my case or ask to rein him in."

"Surely you don't think that I have any influence over Brad. The man may be my son-in-law, true, but we aren't close."

"Oh, no, Jim, I'm not thinking anything like that. I just . . . You've been kindly toward me since I got home.

A lot here aren't. I was just . . . letting off steam, I guess you'd say."

"You could take it up with the town council," Hanson suggested, taking a pencil from a cup on the counter and tearing off a scrap of brown wrapping paper to write on. "We'll call it eighteen cents for the cornmeal." He jotted the figure down.

"That's the thing, Jim. The town council doesn't have any influence over him. The marshal answers only to the people who elected him. Hell, I was one of the fellows who drew up the town charter. We were so proud of ourselves for making the offices separate. Separation of powers and all that. Now I wish your damned son-in-law was answerable to somebody. But he isn't, and he knows it. He can come out to my place any time he wants, as often as he wants. He can paw through my stuff and claim he's looking for stolen goods or he can accuse me of, well, of almost anything he likes."

"But without witnesses to back him up . . ."

"Witnesses would be important if he was going to actually charge me with something, sure. But what the son of a, uh . . ." Wilson looked around, realized that Harriet was in the store and could probably overhear this conversation. "The, uh, son of a toad, what he wants is to push me into doing something that would violate the terms of my parole. Then he could send me back to prison. Tell you the truth, Jim, I'm surprised he hasn't already planted a pistol out at my place and then suddenly found it."

"That would be enough to send you back?" Hanson asked.

"It could. I don't know what sort of hearing he might have to go through or some sort of official action. It's not something I've ever had to think of before now."

"No, I wouldn't suppose so."

"Lyle."

Wilson turned and quickly took his hat off. He nodded to Harriet. "Yes, ma'am?"

"You've bought starches and meats, but what about fruits? You need those for your system, you know. Won't you take some canned peaches with you today? And some dried apples? Raisins too." She smiled. "I know how you bachelors are. You don't take proper care of yourselves."

"That's nice of you to think of me, ma'am." The proprieties having been observed, he put his hat back on and gave the brim a tug to settle it into place.

"You will have some fruits today then, Lyle?"

"Yes, ma'am. Thank you for the suggestion. I'll do just as you say."

Jim Hanson looked relieved that his wife had steered the conversation away from Wilson's troubles with Bradley Thom. He pulled two feet or so of twine off the big spindle beside the counter and with the ease of long practice swiped it down across the cutting edge, a piece of broken razor blade screwed onto the back of the counter. He deftly gathered the top of the cloth sack of cornmeal and wrapped the twine three times around, then tied it tight. "Will you take some fruit?"

"Sure. D'you have anything fresh?"

Hanson shook his head.

"All right. Canned then. How about airtights?"

"I have canning jars."

"No, something bigger. Something that'll keep the varmints out. I don't want t' be overrun with mice in the house. There's enough of them get in the shed. I don't need 'em in the house too."

"I have some tins. They're sized for a couple gallons

or so. Those would do. You could fill them with dried fruits if you like."

"All right. I'll have some of those. Fill them up with whatever you think best. Whatever you think, Harriet." He smiled. "I trust your judgment better than his any day." Wilson turned back to Hanson. "If you don't mind, I'll walk down to the bank while you put the order together. I'm thinking I'll need more cash to cover this now that the load seems to be growing."

"Where is your wagon, Lyle? I'll go ahead and load these things in for you if you like."

"That's mighty nice o' you, Jim. Thanks." Wilson pointed toward the loading dock where he had parked, then he turned in the other direction and headed for the door. He stepped aside and took his hat off again to make way for a pair of nicely dressed ladies who were on their way into the store. As soon as they were well clear of the doorway he went out into the street, still peeved that there was nothing he could do if Marshal Bradley Thom wanted to roust him. After all, Wilson was a convicted felon, free on parole. It was a freedom that seemed less free now than it once had.

CHAPTER TWENTY-SIX

The interior of the Stockman's Bank smelled of new paint and linseed oil but there was no sign of the clutter that usually accompanied refurbishings. They must have been having the work performed through the night so as to keep from annoying customers. There were two people in line at Dave Matthews's teller window ahead of Wilson. He did not know the lady who was conducting her business there at the moment. Charles Darlon, who bought and sold real estate, was next in line.

"Hello, Charlie."

"Hello, Lyle. I heard you were home. It's good to see you." Darlon's smile was broad and his welcome effusive. Wilson was taken somewhat aback. He and Darlon had never gotten along particularly well in the past.

"It's good to be back, Charlie."

"When you have the time," Darlon said, "you might stop by my office. There's something I'd like to discuss with you. But not here if you don't mind." Darlon glanced around as if afraid someone might overhear their conversation.

"Thank you, David. You have a fine day now, you hear?" The lady in front of them completed her bank business, draped the strap of her bag over her forearm and left.

Darlon glanced back at Wilson. "When you're done here? Would that be convenient?"

"Sure, Charlie. I suppose so."

Darlon nodded, turned back toward Matthews's window and stepped forward. Wilson remained where he was. Whatever Charlie's banking business was, he did not want to know about it.

Whatever it was it took only a few moments to conduct. When Darlon stepped away from the teller's window he paused and in a very low voice barely above a whisper said, "I'll be waiting in my office, Lyle. When you're done here, eh?"

"Sure, Charlie." Wilson smiled. "We'll talk."

Darlon hunched his shoulders and scurried away, looking for all the world like a man with secrets to keep, Wilson thought. Not that he particularly cared. He did not like Charles Darlon well enough to share either his secrets or his burdens.

"What can I do for you today?" Matthews asked with a smile as Wilson approached his teller window.

"I just need a withdrawal slip, Dave." He looked around. There was no one waiting behind him. "I'll just fill it out here if you don't mind."

"Tell me how much you want and I can get it for you while you're doing that," Matthews offered. "Will I need to go to the vault or get Mr. Fredericks's approval first?"

"Oh, no. Nothing like that. I just want some walking-around cash."

"Then I should have it in my drawer," Matthews said. He pushed a printed slip beneath the cage. "Fill out the amount you want, Lyle, and sign for it, please."

CHAPTER TWENTY-SEVEN

Wilson stepped outside and absentmindedly pulled the bank's door shut behind him. At the sound of Wilson's footsteps a striped yellow cat ran out from beneath the boards of the sidewalk. It spooked a dray horse that was standing at the side of the street and nearly got itself stomped. The horse stamped its feet, snorted once and settled down; the cat escaped to the river side of the block and disappeared into an alley there. Wilson grunted his pleasure at being able to observe such small and unimportant details of normal life. Life without bars. Life without the stultifying sameness of unvarying routine. Life without walls and watchtowers and armed guards. Normal life. It was more beautiful than he had ever realized before his conviction.

Smiling, he started up the sidewalk. He reached inside his coat for his wallet, brought it out and spread it open. He folded the bills he had withdrawn from his account and stuffed them into a pocket in the wallet, then returned the somewhat worn and battered black leather wallet to his inside coat pocket. As he did so he stepped down from the sidewalk and strode across the mouth of a narrow alley.

"Psst."

Wilson stopped. Paused there in the mouth of the alley.

"Yeah, dammit. You."

He turned his head. The man lurking in the alley was a stranger to him. But then so many in Fox Hill were these days. They were people who had arrived after he went away, and many others who had been his friends or at least were familiar to him had gone and he did not know where.

This fellow was fairly tall, at least three inches taller than Wilson. He was burly, with wide shoulders and powerfully muscled arms. He had a protruding belly that hung over his belt. He had not shaved in some days; dark stubble peppered his neck and cheeks. Beneath the beard his face was crisscrossed with lines of scarring from past conflicts. He was hatless, his hair unkempt and tangled. He did not appear to be armed, but Wilson did not doubt the man in the alley could overpower him in a fight. Or thought he could anyway. Wilson had learned a thing or two while he was in prison. One of the things he had learned was to never back down. Never.

He turned to face the fellow and marched directly to him. He demanded, "Is there something you want, mister, 'cause I'm no damned virgin."

"Whoa. Hey, now." The fellow held his hands shoulder high with his palms outward. "Slow down. I'm not . . . That is to say . . . I'm not looking for no trouble. I want t' talk to you, that's all."

Wilson remained poised to lash out. The fellow said he was not looking for trouble. That did not mean anything. Men had been known to lie before now. Lie to Wilson. And lie about him. This fellow . . . his intentions remained to be seen. "If you don't want trouble, what is it that you do want?"

"Look, I, uh . . . My name is Marble. John Marble,

but everybody calls me Stony. You're Lyle Wilson, right?"

Wilson nodded. He was still ready for a fight if that was what Stony Marble had in mind.

"Yeah. Right. An' I hear you done some time in the gray stone college."

"So what! Lots of fellows do," Wilson responded.

"Right. Lots of us. Me, I done time. Here. Up in Colorado. Once in Alabama. That's the worst. Stay outa trouble in Alabama if you ever get the chance."

"Thanks for the advice," Wilson said, his voice drily sarcastic. "I'll try and do that little thing. Was there something else?"

"Yeah, I, uh, my partner and me got something planned. We could use a third hand. Just for a lookout, mind. Nothing fancy. You wouldn't even have t' carry a gun. I don't carry one myself. See?" He turned around, surprisingly light on his feet for a man of his size, and slapped his sides to invite inspection. Stony turned back around to face Wilson again. "You wouldn't get a full share. Understand that. We'd be taking most of the risk and we'd keep most o' the take. But we'd take care o' you. You got my word on that. We—"

Wilson held his hand up to stop Stony from telling him anything more. "I don't wanta know about it. Whatever it is, keep it to yourself. If it goes wrong I don't want you thinking maybe I said something to somebody and it got back to the wrong people. So don't tell me."

"But you—"

"I'm not interested, Stony. Whatever it is, I'm not interested. I mean that."

"You got your own thing going here, is that it, Wilson?"

"I'm just . . . Leave be. That's all. Just leave be."

"Sure. Whatever you say, Wilson. But listen. You look like you're a guy as has some smarts. If you come up with anything that needs another hand or two, you look me up. I'll be around." He grinned, exposing a gap in his upper teeth. "For a while anyhow."

"Good luck, Stony."

"Yeah. You too, Wilson. Whatever it is you're up to, I wish you good luck with it. An' I mean that sincerely." Marble turned and disappeared into the alley, his shoulders so broad they filled the narrow space.

Wilson paused there. His heart was racing and he had begun to sweat profusely. He took several long, slow, deliberate breaths, forced himself to thoroughly exhale before he breathed in again, then started back toward Jim Hanson's general store.

CHAPTER TWENTY-EIGHT

Lyle Wilson was only now beginning to understand what his own reputation had become in and around Fox Hill. He was, very simply, viewed as a convicted felon. That seemed to be the one thing that even total strangers understood about him.

Thieves like Stony Marble looked to him now as a fellow thief. Honest townspeople looked at him as something apart from themselves. Something beneath themselves. No wonder the men who gathered in his once-favorite café did not want to eat or to drink coffee with him. He was no longer one of them.

And there was not a damn thing he could do to change any of that.

Wilson walked the rest of the way back to Jim Hanson's store at a slow pace. The weight of the world lay on his shoulders. Or so he felt.

The prison walls were not as far behind him as he had thought they were.

"Is something wrong, Lyle? You look down," Hanson said when he entered the store.

Wilson shook his head. "I'm all right, Jim, but thanks for asking." He raised his chin up and forced a smile that he did not really feel. "Everything all right here?"

"Oh, yes. Your wagon is all loaded. Your dry commodities are in big cookie tins. Rice, cornmeal, flour and like that. You'll have to look inside to see what each one is and then store them so that you know which is which. But there won't be any mouse that's man enough to chew their way into them."

"That sounds fine, Jim, thanks."

"Are you sure you're all right?"

"Yeah. Really. How much do I owe you?"

"It comes to . . . wait a minute, I wrote it down somewhere . . . right. Here it is. Twelve sixty-seven."

"That covers everything?"

"Everything except my sweat getting it out to your wagon," Hanson told him with another smile.

"Look, Jim, I—" Wilson cut the sentence short as the front door opened and Sarah came into her father's store.

Wilson ducked his head, his mood immediately reverting to the misery that had accompanied him in here. He clenched his jaw and headed out the side door toward the loading dock, where his wagon stood.

He did not speak to Sarah and did not even say good-bye to the man who, if things had been different, might have been his father-in-law.

CHAPTER TWENTY-NINE

Wilson unclipped the hitch weight from the bay's snaffle and set the weight onto the floor of the driving box, but instead of climbing onto the seat, he stood in the street, leaning against the side of the wagon, his thoughts far from the moment at hand.

He truly did not know what to do, which way to turn. Four years ago, before all of this, there would have been no question about any of it. Four years ago Lyle Wilson would have marched into the town marshal's office and told Jim Tubb what Stony and his unnamed friend had in mind. Or anyway told him what little Lyle knew about the plan.

Now . . . Now Bradley Thom was marshal of Fox Hill. Wilson was fairly certain if he came up with information about a proposed theft—which this most assuredly had to be—Thom would arrest him along with Stony Marble. Plus maybe the other fellow too, in the unlikely event that Thom could figure out who the third man was.

Any connection between Lyle Wilson and a crime, any connection and any crime, would be enough for Thom to have him sent back to prison.

One of the many lessons Wilson learned when he was in Stone Wall College was that one inmate does not snitch on another.

But dammit, he was not an inmate. Not any longer. He wanted . . . More than anything Wilson wanted to go back to the way things used to be here in this town he had chosen as his home. He wanted to be an ordinary citizen with all the usual rights and privileges that came with such a feeling. Rights, privileges and responsibilities, he reminded himself. One of which was to protect his fellow citizens from harm of every sort.

He took a deep breath and ran his hand lightly over the massive hip of the bay mare. Walked forward to her shoulder and used his fingers to comb through her mane, then straightened her forelock and smoothed it down.

"What do we do, girl? Any suggestions?"

Damned horse didn't answer.

"Lyle. Are you all right?"

Wilson glanced back toward the store where Hanson stood on the loading dock.

"Sure, Jim, I was just . . . just woolgathering. Guess I'm blocking your dock. Sorry."

"You know I don't mind you parking there for as long as you like. I just wanted to make sure you're all right."

"Fine, Jim. Thanks."

"All right then. I'll see you next time."

"Right. Next time."

Hanson wiped his hands on his apron, nodded to Lyle and went back indoors.

Wilson grunted, then climbed onto the box of his wagon. He picked up his lines and took a light contact with the mouth of the mare. "Let's go, girl," he said with a shake of the leathers.

He knew where he was going. He even knew—more or less—what he would do when he got there.

CHAPTER THIRTY

Wilson snapped his fingers, impatient with himself, and pulled his wagon to a halt. He pursed his lips and gave a shrill whistle, attracting the attention of the few townspeople who were on the street. Wilson pointed to a rather raggedy towhead who looked like he might be ten or eleven, then crooked his finger to beckon the boy near.

The kid looked skeptical. But he came, stopping beside the off wheel of Lyle Wilson's wagon. "Yes, sir?"

"Do you know Charles Darlon, son?"

"Yes, sir. Reckon I do."

"Know where his office is?"

"Yes, sir."

"Could you take a message to him for me?"

"Yes, sir, I might could." The boy tossed his head to throw back a hank of hair that had fallen into his eyes.

"Do you know me?"

The boy shook his head. "No, sir, I don't."

"My name is Wilson. Would you repeat that for me, please." The boy did. "Lyle Wilson. I told Mr. Darlon I'd stop by his office this afternoon, but I'm not going to be able to do that. I'd like you to tell him I'm sorry but I'll come by another time." Wilson stuffed a hand into his pants pocket and came out with some coins. He pushed a finger through them, rejecting the yellow ones and separating the small coins to one side of his palm. His fingers hovered over a two-cent piece, then a nickel, finally settling on a dime. "Here you go. Mind now. Tell Mr. Darlon that Lyle Wilson will come see him some other time but not today."

"Yes, sir, I got that." The boy reached up and rather eagerly snatched the silver coin out of Wilson's grasp. He grinned hugely, spun around and set off at a run toward Darlon's real-estate office.

Wilson took up his lines again and spoke softly to the bay. He pulled left, stopped to allow a dray to go past and wheeled back toward Main, then right, but instead of continuing on toward the turnoff to his place, Wilson drove under the trees beside the Protestant church and stopped there.

He sat on the wagon seat, reluctant to step down but hoping someone would notice his arrival and come out to see why he was there in the middle of the week. That did not happen, so with a deep breath and a sigh, Wilson climbed down to the ground.

The front door was not locked—he doubted it ever had been in all the time this church existed—and opened easily to him.

Wilson's footsteps rang loud on the sanctuary floor. He tried to tread as softly as possible so as not to make so much noise. He stopped just inside the twin doors and left the one door standing open lest anyone think he was sneaking around. "Hello?" There was no response, so he tried again, louder. "Hello? Is anyone here?"

It was almost a relief when there was no response.

At the front of the church, flanking the altar on either side of the building, were two very small rooms. One held the choir's robes. Those, he well remembered after the dissent that had once threatened to divide the little congregation, were ordinary cotton yard goods that the ladies of the church had dyed and sewn themselves. The women's Bible group had done that as a project one winter. An opposing and very vocal faction in the church had felt that a set of red satin robes should be ordered from a catalog house in Massachusetts. The church board decided—after weeks of discussion that fringed upon outright argument—that the satin robes would be nice but were too expensive. For the moment. The plain robes, dark green instead of the fancier red, hung now in the cloakroom. That probably was a discussion that would be held again someday, when a larger congregation was contributing to the church budget.

Opposite that room, on the left or westernmost side of the church, was the pastor's study. The door to it was closed at the moment, and likely Pastor Moore was out somewhere.

Now that he was there, Wilson was not sure if he hoped Moore was inside his study . . . or not.

He was there, though, and he might as well find out if the pastor was present.

Wilson took a deep breath and marched up the center aisle, letting his footsteps ring as loud as they pleased.

CHAPTER THIRTY-ONE

Wilson felt a tremendous relief when he yanked the door open and found . . . an empty room. Nothing more than that. No Pastor Moore. Nothing but a small, bare writing table with a cloth-bound hymnal on it, a slim sheaf of foolscap, an ink bottle with a white quill protruding from it and a tiny window set high in the side wall. A wooden stool was pushed beneath the table. Presumably Moore sat there while writing his sermons. There were no adornments. The room seemed no more comfortable than Wilson's cell had been. Less so. At least his cell had had a bunk and mattress. The pastor's study lacked even that.

Wilson considered leaving a note, then changed his mind. He should mind his own business. He was not his brother's keeper. Except, dammit, he was. He remembered that passage, and that was the whole point of the thing. We are too our brothers' keepers, and the good people of Fox Hill were his brothers. So to speak.

Wilson sighed again and, grumbling silently to himself, entered the study. He hooked a toe behind one leg of the stool and drew it out from beneath the table, sat down and slid a sheet of the cheap foolscap from the pile. He pulled it in front of him and took the quill out of the ink bottle so he could begin writing.

"What the . . . ?" A frown creased Wilson's forehead as he stared at the tip of the quill.

There was no nib. No modern steel nib inserted into the end of the shaft and not even a nib shape whittled into the natural goose feather. Some ink darkened the blunt tip, but there was no way this quill could be used to write with.

Wilson's frown deepened to a scowl when a drop of ink fell off the end of the quill onto the pastor's writing table. It splattered into a dozen tiny droplets when it hit.

"Dammit." He dropped the useless quill back into the bottle, folded his sheet of foolscap and used the paper to blot up the spillage lest it leave a permanent stain. He polished the table with the paper, then folded it over several times more and stuffed the resulting wad into his pocket. Thoroughly disgruntled, he stood and used the side of his foot to push the stool back underneath the table where he had found it.

He turned to leave.

And found himself face-to-face with a young woman. Well, nose to forehead if not exactly face-to-face. She had to be at least half a foot shorter than he. No, more. If he had been pressed up against her, his chin would easily have cleared the top of her head.

The image of himself pressing against her leaped into his mind and stuck there. It would not have seemed a bad idea, actually. She was . . . she was pretty. And Lyle Wilson was not accustomed to encountering attractive young women. He was somewhat out of practice.

He would have been willing to relearn the social niceties with this one to teach him.

She was a tiny slip of a thing, both short of stature and very slight of build. She seemed scarcely big enough to qualify as a grown person except that she was clearly no child.

Wisps of strawberry blonde hair escaped from a large, floppy sunbonnet that framed a face dominated by clear, bright blue eyes. A spray of freckles lay across the bridge of a pert, somewhat pointed nose. Her lips were full. And very red. Her teeth small and very white. She had long, curling eyelashes. High cheekbones. Pale eyebrows. Eyes that . . .

He kept coming back to her eyes. Wilson could scarcely take his eyes away from hers.

He should say something. He knew that. He should say . . . what?

Instead he stood mute, shifted from one foot to the other and back again. Felt his palms begin to become moist with anxiety. He opened his mouth, but to gulp for air rather than to speak.

The woman smiled. "Hello."

Wilson nodded.

"Are you a parishioner?"

He nodded again.

Her smile became wider. "I don't believe I've met you yet." She put a hand forward to shake, which very gently he did. "I'm Eva Moore."

Moore. The same as Pastor Moore. Of course. The pastor's wife. Lordy, what a lucky man Moore was. And her name was Eva, his Evan. Tidy.

The knowledge snapped Wilson out of the stupor the appearance of this young woman caused. "I'm, uh, here to see Pastor Moore. But he isn't in. So I . . . I'm pleased to meet you. I'll be on my way now. Thank you. Good-bye."

Before Wilson could escape Eva touched his wrist. He could have sworn he felt a shock when she did, the same sort of shock one got in winter from scuffing your feet along a carpet and then touching something metal. But there was no carpet in here to build a charge on.

"Don't leave. Evan is over at the parsonage. Do you know where it is?"

He shook his head. The church had not owned a parsonage when he went away. Apparently that was one of the many changes that had taken place since.

"I saw your wagon outside," Eva said. "That's why I stopped in. Would you like me to show you to the parsonage? It isn't far. I could ride with you. Or we could walk, whichever you would rather."

"It isn't far, you say?"

"Just on the next block over."

Wilson said, "Best to leave the horse where it is then. Out of the way, I mean. But I don't want to bother you."

"Oh, it's no bother. Not at all. Come along then." She smiled again, took him by the elbow and led him toward the door of the pastor's study.

CHAPTER THIRTY-TWO

Eva Moore chattered away like they were old friends catching up after a long separation. She liked hominy and sugar-cured ham, liked to get up before daybreak so she could watch the sun come up on a chilly morning, liked to fish but had to leave her pole behind when they moved to Fox Hill. She and Evan had moved to Arizona Territory from North Carolina.

Back home everyone warned them against coming into such unsettled territory where there could be brigands and wild Indians and all sorts of other dangers. She was almost disappointed to find that Fox Hill was so quiet and civilized, with not a marauder in sight and not a single shootout in all the time they had been here. In fact, Fox Hill seemed little different from their village back home.

"Disappointed?" Lyle asked.

"That the town is quiet and civil and nice?" Eva laughed. "To be honest . . . perhaps a little disappointed, yes. I thought moving to a place that wasn't even a state . . . I thought that would be, well, romantic. And just a little bit dangerous. Why, can you believe it, the few Indians I've seen have been more pitiable than scary. And I've never met a single outlaw." She laughed again and tossed her head. "Every little girl has daydreams about a dashing young road agent who will

sweep her off her feet and carry her away to a life of . . ."
Eva began to blush, her cheeks and her ears practically
aglow with bright red.

"A life of what?" Lyle asked.

"Oh, you know."

"Matter of fact, I don't know. I've never been a little
girl, you see."

Eva laughed again, and as she relaxed, the redness
in her cheeks began to subside. "It isn't important."

"Maybe you'll tell me someday," he suggested.

"Perhaps. But I doubt it." She stopped and pointed
to a narrow gate in a low picket fence. "This is where
we live. This is the parsonage."

A man named Hooper used to live there, Lyle recalled. A wheelwright. Behind his back everyone called
him Hooper the Cooper, but the gentleman had no
sense of humor and did not welcome levity of any sort,
and all the less so if the joking was at his expense.

Wilson had no idea what might have happened to
Hooper—he could not remember the man's first name,
just that silly "Hooper the Cooper" nickname—whether
he died or simply moved away. He had lived alone in
Fox Hill, although rumor had it that he once had a
wife back wherever he came from. Somewhere in New
England, Lyle thought. Hooper never spoke of a wife,
if indeed he had one or once did.

The house was tiny, built on a single small lot. Every
lot in town had been surveyed and platted, but the lots
were all rather narrow at only twenty feet, and most
people purchased two or even three before they built.
Hooper was one of the few who had chosen to estab-
lish themselves on a single town lot.

Lyle opened the gate and held it for Eva to pass
through, then carefully closed and latched it back again.

He surreptitiously peered at the girl as she passed practically under his nose in order to get through the narrow gate while he held it for her.

He could catch her scent. Or thought he could.

Her throat was so delicate. He saw a tracery of blood vessels faint beneath the pink softness of her flesh, and his body began to respond to her closeness in a most unwelcome way. Wilson practically jumped back to get farther away from her.

Eva tilted her head and looked up at him from beneath the brim of her bonnet. "I don't bite, you know."

"No, uh, of course not," he stammered. "Look ahere now, there's something you should ought to know about me."

She stopped on the flagstone walkway that led to the front porch of the parsonage. "Yes?"

"I'm . . . That is . . . a person could say that, well, in a way . . . in a way I guess you've met an outlaw after all. Or anyhow a jailbird. I'm—"

"Oh, I know who you are, Mr. Wilson. And what you are. You were pointed out to me. Now come along and we'll see if we can find Evan." Eva took off her bonnet and shook her head to fluff her curls, then mounted the two steps up to the porch and pulled the screened door open, standing there holding it open with one hand while her bonnet dangled by its strings from the other. "Come along then, if you're going to."

Wilson snapped his jaw closed—he was sure it was hanging open after that surprise—and scampered to join her.

CHAPTER THIRTY-THREE

Wilson had never been inside the little house when Hooper still lived there, but the floor plan seemed simple enough. It was what was termed a shotgun structure, with each room occupying the full width of the building and the rooms constructed one after another, front to back. The house was perhaps sixteen feet wide. The front room, and presumably each succeeding room behind it, about eight feet. The front room was the main living area, furnished with rocking chairs and a settee. And with bookshelves. Wherever there was wall space there were shelves filled to overflowing with books. There was also a writing table with a lamp suspended above it and an assortment of pencils, pens and ink beneath the hanging lamp.

The next room back, judging from the glimpse Wilson got through the open doorway, would be the kitchen. He could, at any rate, see what looked like a kitchen table with chairs in that room.

Past the kitchen he had no way to know how many other rooms there might be, bedrooms more than likely, and in back there should be a utility area, either a room or a porch where laundry could be washed or scraps collected or the like.

Eva stepped inside and with an impish glance back

toward Wilson loudly said, "Evan dear, our resident desperado has come to see you."

"Who?" The pastor appeared in the kitchen doorway. He was frowning. He had a book in one hand and a coffee cup in the other. His expression brightened. "Wilson. Good. But Eva, I thought you said . . ." He laughed. "I gather you meant Mr. Wilson here when you said something about a desperado. Mr. Wilson, you must forgive her, please. Eva often forgets that not everyone shares her sense of humor. Sometimes I don't myself, even after all these years." Moore set his coffee cup down on a nearby plant stand and crossed the room with his free hand extended. "It's good to see you, Lyle. Sit down. Please. Eva, bring Mr. Wilson some coffee, if you please. How do you take it, Lyle?"

"Oh, I don't want to be a bo—"

"It's no bother. Really. Eva made a fresh pot just before she started for town. I couldn't possibly drink it all by myself. Some would be wasted if you won't join me."

"I . . . All right. Milk if you have it. And a little sugar."

"Just the way I take my coffee," Eva said. She dropped her bag and bonnet onto the seat of a battered old rocking chair and brushed past Moore into the kitchen. Wilson dropped into the chair that had been offered to him. Moore retrieved his cup from the plant stand and put his book aside. He selected a seat close by Wilson.

The pastor leaned forward and set his coffee aside again, his hands on his knees and his expression intense. "What is it that has brought you here, Lyle? What can I do for you?"

CHAPTER THIRTY-FOUR

Lyle felt better when he walked away from the parsonage. He did not owe Fox Hill a damned thing, but he had done his civic duty to the best of his ability in spite of that. Pastor Moore could in good conscience tip Marshal Thom to the threat of a nighttime break-in—which Lyle had concluded the plan had to be, otherwise Stony would not have emphasized a distaste for the use of guns—yet keep Lyle's name from ever coming up. Lyle would not be associated with the plan in any way. And that was just the way he wanted it.

He crossed through a vacant lot, the weeds and low brush whipping at his pant legs, and then through an alley to get to Main. A stagecoach rumbled past with a clatter of hoofbeats, the creak of leather and a jangle of trace chain. The jehu, a man Lyle had never seen before, gave him a friendly wave in passing. Everyone in Fox Hill used to do that, Lyle reflected, the memory sending a pang of regret through his chest. Now . . . very few even wanted to speak with him.

He still did have a few friends though. That thought cheered him a little. Some of the businessmen still welcomed him, of course. Lyle himself or his money, but the fact was that they welcomed him. A good many of the folks who attended the church were friendly enough too. And of course there were the Moores, Evan and Eva.

Lordy, that Eva was a cute little button. She seemed a perfect companion for Evan, both of them small and active.

Lyle felt another, sharper pang when he thought now about Sarah. Thought about Sarah and what might have been. Might have been but was not.

He sighed. Sarah Hanson had become Sarah Thom now, wedded and bedded and twice a mother of Bradley Thom's get.

Damn her!

Lyle reached his parked wagon on the church grounds. Blindly he grabbed up the hitch weight and threw it under the seat, then stepped on the axle and on up into the box. He picked up the lines and barely took time enough to sort them into his fingers before he was hauling on them to back the mare away. He turned her head and clucked to her and began to roll.

The mare was still too new to trust to find her own way home. She was as apt to head for the livery as for Wilson's corral. That or for wherever it was she came from before Sam Arnold acquired her. A few months of being fed inside that corral and she would associate it with the home place. Then he could get her started on her way, wrap the lines around the whip socket and go to sleep while the mare found her own way back. But not now. Not yet.

Lyle sat tall on the seat. He had as good as no pride left after the years inside. That prison had broken him and he knew it. But be damned if he would let anyone in Fox Hill see that in him. He might not have any pride remaining, but another thing he had learned inside was to never back down. Never.

CHAPTER THIRTY-FIVE

Wilson had company waiting when he got home, old Pablo Montez, who normally would be selling burritos down beside the bridge, and a Mexican man he did not believe he had ever seen before. The newcomer was a tall, dignified-looking fellow, not as old as Pablo but with a good many years on him. He had some gray in his mustache and in the shaggy mane that showed beneath his sombrero.

The two were waiting on Wilson's front porch. They stood and came down to take the horse by the bit and hold her while Wilson climbed down. Both helped Wilson to unload his supplies onto the porch; then Pablo helped him carry everything inside while the stranger unhitched the mare and led her first to the water trough and then into the corral, where he expertly stripped the harness from her, sorted it out and draped it onto the fence posts.

"What can I do for you today, Pablo?" Wilson asked once everything was piled inside. He could sort through it later and decide what should go where. He smiled. "I don't have any more furniture here than I do outside. What do you say we go set on the edge of the porch to talk. First, though, can I put a pot o' coffee on for you and your friend?"

"We are fine, senor. We drank of your good water while we waited for you to come home."

Wilson trailed his visitor out onto the porch and down to the ground, then perched beside him on the forward edge of the platform. He waited. Pablo would get to the reason for the visit in his own good time.

Pablo's friend was busying himself out by the corral even though he was long since done with the simple chore of putting the mare up.

"I have had a thought," Pablo announced after several minutes of silence had gone by.

Wilson nodded and continued to peer off toward the silver gleam of the distant Fox River.

"You have no cattle," Pablo observed.

"That's right. I'll be looking to restock soon, I suppose. Have to buy some more horses first. See if I can find someone who will sell me some hay. Things like that. I'll be ready by and by, but to tell you the truth, Pablo, by then it will be late enough in the year that it won't make no sense to buy cattle. I'll likely be better off to wait for springtime, then look to restock. I'll not be hiring any hands, if that's what you are thinking. First because there's no need for it now and won't be for quite a spell an' secondly because I just plain can't afford hired help. Time I pay for a herd of breeding stock I'll be pretty well cleaned out. I'm telling you the God's natural truth, Pablo."

"I believe you, Senor Lyle. It is not this that we came for." The old man pulled a pipe from his pocket and took his time about loading and lighting it. Wilson waited for Montez to decide that he was ready to say his piece.

Out by the corral the other Mexican had given up pretending to be busy. He was just standing there, leaning his crossed forearms on the top fence rail and with one sandal propped up on the bottom rail.

"My friend," Pablo said finally, "he is Luis Santiago, of him I have mentioned to you."

It took Wilson a moment to bring the name back to mind, then he nodded. "Of course. He manages the goats for Anders Donovan, right?"

Pablo nodded. "*Si*, senor. Exactly so."

"But he's out of a job now because Donovan is selling off his goats," Wilson recalled.

"*Si*. Senor Donovan is selling everything. He has horses too, you know. And sheep. Many sheep. Not so many goats. He has not had the goats so very long like he has the sheep."

"Right. So I recall."

"He is selling his land. He will go to Texas, where he has a daughter. He will spend his last years with her. Play with his grandbabies. Teach them to play tricks on their brothers. He says he is getting old, as we all will if God smiles on us. He says he wants to enjoy them while he still has the health to do so. He is a wise man, I think, this Senor Donovan."

"Yes, I'd say that he is, Pablo. And fortunate to have family." The comment caused a moment of discomfort for Wilson, who was reminded that he himself would probably never have wife or children, either one.

"Luis, he knows goats. Knows where to sell the wool from the *cabra*. Where to sell the milk. Goat's milk is very good for the little ones, you know. For human babies. Very easy on their stomach. Babies who often have the colic, they need the milk of the *cabra*. Luis sells it to them for Senor Donovan."

"I didn't know that," Wilson said.

"*Si*. And you know about the meat of the kid."

"Oh, I sure know about that."

"What I say to Luis is that maybe so it is a good thing that Senor Donovan will sell his flock."

"How's that, Pablo?"

"Maybe it will be so that a man who has land but has no cattle will want to buy this flock from Senor Donovan. And Luis will stay with his goats to work for this other man."

"Could happen, I reckon."

"The goats, they do not make much money but what they do make, it is . . ." Pablo paused and flapped his hands."

"Regular?" Wilson suggested.

"*Si*. Regular. All the year around. Except for the wool. That is only in the spring of the year. But milk and meat, those are to be sold all the year. Not much money." He grinned. "But regular. Good for a man who is not greedy."

"I can see how that would be."

"Luis does not ask much pay, senor. A little only. And half of the female offspring. Half of the increase. Because Luis has the thought to one day have his own flock. You know the story of Jacob? He tended the sheep for Laban. He received part of the increase of that flock and in time he was a rich man with flock of his own."

"I remember," Wilson said. Sort of. He had not heard any of those stories since he was a child sitting on a hard bench in Sunday school.

"What Luis has in mind would be the same." Pablo laughed. "But without the cheating."

Wilson did not remember any cheating in that story, but then he did not really remember those Old Testament stories very well to begin with. He chuckled along with Pablo's laugh and let it go at that. "I think that sounds like a good plan, Pablo," he ventured. "Could be good for everybody. The owner of the herd makes some money plus increases his own herd, and at the same time Luis builds up a herd of his own. Yeah, I kind of like that idea. If you can find the right buyer, that is. Somebody that'll go along with that idea."

"We think we have found the man who would be so very good to work for."

"If only this fella will buy the goats off Donovan," Wilson said. "And if him and Donovan can agree on a price."

Pablo's grin occupied half his grizzled face. "Oh, Luis has already spoken with Senor Donovan and the price is very small. Compared to cows it is. Very small."

Pablo stood and waved for Luis to come join them. He turned to Wilson and, still grinning, said, "Luis is an honest man. He will never cheat you, Senor Lyle."

"Me? But I—"

Wilson's protestations were lost in an exuberant gushing of joy as Luis Santiago came running to stand before Wilson, drop to his knees and begin kissing Wilson's hands.

Goats. What the hell did he know about goats? And he wished Luis would quit slobbering on his hands. It was embarrassing, dammit.

CHAPTER THIRTY-SIX

Wilson stood and leaned across the table to shake Anders Donovan's hand. "Good luck in Texas. I hope you have many years to enjoy your family there."

The older man nodded. "Thanks. An' I hope you do well with your flock. You can count on Luis. He's a good man. Knows his job. Hell, he even collects the money that comes in from selling this 'n that. Collects it and marks a tally stick so's he can give an accounting when he turns it over to me. Which he's always been faithful about."

"He uses a tally stick?"

"Oh, yes. The man can't read nor write a lick, but he's honest as the day is long. About once every couple months he'll drive the goats down to the home place— that'll be your outfit now—an' turn over whatever money he's collected. He'll set down so's you can write out a list of the things he needs. It'll be up t' you then to buy the supplies he tells you an' deliver them up to them. Give me a minute now, Lyle. I need t' write out your bill o' sale. We want everything t' be nice an' legal."

Donovan fetched out ink, an assortment of pens and a folder of good-quality linen paper. He cleared his throat, brought a pair of spectacles out of his pocket and bent over the paper to make out the bill of sale.

In addition to the goats—942 of them, according to a count made the day before—Wilson was buying a sheepherder's caravan, two large and rather ugly dogs, the pair of mottled brown cobs that pulled the wagon and whatever supplies were in it. He was also, and most importantly, acquiring the services of Luis.

Donovan signed the document and handed it—and with it, ownership of the herd—to Wilson; then the two men walked outside to where Luis was waiting on the porch. Donovan shook Santiago's hand and said, "You 're a good man, Luis. Good luck."

"And to you, senor." Luis turned to Wilson and said, "Do you have instruction, jefe?"

"No, Luis." Wilson smiled. "Let's go home."

Santiago nodded. "*Bueno*. I will see you there in one month. Maybe two." He turned, climbed onto his wagon and drove away without a backward look.

"There goes a man who is at peace with his world," Donovan said.

"We should all be so lucky."

The older man started to speak, closed his mouth again and appeared to be in thought.

"Something on your mind, Anders?" Wilson asked.

"We don't know each other very good, Lyle. No reason for that that I can think of except that we haven't lived close nor spent time in the same towns. I've never got over to Fox Hill all that often, an' you haven't come over here much."

"True."

"But I've always liked you, Lyle. It surprised me when they said what they did about you. Surprised me all the more to find out you'd done it."

Wilson stifled an impulse to protest. No one ever believed him when he claimed his innocence.

"I always believe a man should ought to be given a second chance though." Donovan cleared his throat. "Not, uh . . . not everyone thinks that way."

"Are you trying to tell me something, Anders?"

"I am. I'm saying that I've heard rumors. There's someone over to Fox Hill that has it in for you. They want you out o' the way. Might have t' do with land an' politics an' all that." He cleared his throat again and spat. "Then again it might be nothin' at all. Just rumor an' wild talk. It, uh . . . it come t' my mind that a man like you, with a prison record an' all, might be an easy target if somebody wanted t' get him in trouble. 'Specially if he was on parole. You know what I mean?"

Wilson felt a chill slither up his spine. He nodded. "Yes, Anders, I'm afraid I do know what you mean. Thanks for telling me."

"I don't mean t' worry you. An' it could be nothing at all. But I thought, well, I thought you ought for to know."

"Thanks. Thank you more than I can say."

"Good luck to you, Lyle."

"And to you, Anders."

The two men shook hands again. Then Wilson reclaimed his mare from the hitch rail and stepped onto her saddle, having left the wagon at home for the ride over to Donovan's place.

He was deep in thought before he ever cleared Donovan's yard.

CHAPTER THIRTY-SEVEN

Evan Moore buttonholed Wilson after services the following Sunday morning. "I'd like to speak with you, Lyle, but away from all the bustle and commotion of the after-church picnics if you don't mind."

"Of course. It's fine with me." He grinned. "Although today I remembered to bring something to contribute to the communal table. Brought some of my world-famous baked beans for all to enjoy."

"That famous, are they?"

"If they aren't, they ought to be."

The pastor said, "I'm pretty much obligated to stay here for the meal today, Lyle, but if you don't mind driving back in to town, perhaps you could come by tomorrow evening and take your supper with Eva and me."

"Did I hear my name mentioned here?" Eva had been walking past, but she stopped and came back to stand beside Moore. She linked her arm through his and tilted her head to one side so she could peer up at him past the brim of her bonnet.

"You did. I was just telling Lyle here that you aren't a very good cook but I've been able to recover from every meal you've ever cooked for me. Recover eventually, anyway."

Eva poked him in the ribs and Evan winced. "Did

you remember to invite him to decide for himself
about my cooking?" she demanded, knuckles poised
for another assault on his ribs if she did not like his
answer.

"I did. And he said he'll come."

Eva was all smiles at that news. "Good." She turned
to Wilson. "Supper then? About six?"

Lyle nodded. "Fine. I'll be there." To Evan he added,
"And thank you for the invitation." He understood it
was proper to thank the husband in these matters
even though it was the wife who would be doing all
the work involved. He thought that seemed a strange
custom, but it was what was expected.

Wilson excused himself and went out to his wagon
to get the pot of beans he baked on his brand-new
sheepherder's stove. They were the first serious cooking
he had done—cooking for others to eat, that is—and he
was nervous about how they would be received. At
least the crazy stovetop contraption that was supposed
to substitute for a real oven had done its job, because the
beans were cooked yet did not seem to have been
burned onto the bottom of his pan the way he had
feared they might.

He lifted the lid off the pan and filched a piece of the
bacon he had used as one of the seasoning ingredients.
He chewed on that, enjoying the flavor, while he carried his world-famous beans around to the picnic area
in the grove behind the church.

The folks were gathered. It was a beautiful Sunday
afternoon. What could be nicer?

CHAPTER THIRTY-EIGHT

Wilson smiled. The tall gentleman who had invited him to eat with them was back today, and the baskets his boys were carrying looked temptingly heavy. "Hello again," he said. "Is that invitation still open?"

"What inv—? Oh, yes. Of course."

"I brought something to contribute to the table today," Wilson said.

"Not that it was necessary, but I do understand." The man extended his hand. "I'm Leonard Keng. This is my wife Liza. Our sons there are Kyle and Eddie."

"Eddie is the Keng with the dirty face," Liza added, "which he was told to keep clean until we get home and he can change out of his good clothes." She patiently tugged the drawstring of her reticule, opened it and dug inside for a moment, coming out with a small, lace-edged handkerchief. The lady held the kerchief to her face, pursed her lips and spat on a corner of the cloth, which she then used to scrub a large, dark smudge off Eddie's left cheek.

"Ma!" Eddie protested. "Not here." But Wilson noticed that he did not try to squirm away, no matter how unwelcome his mother's attentions might be in this time and place.

"Come along, Lyle," Keng said, genuine welcome in

his voice. "There's a particularly soft and grassy spot over here where we like to spread our blanket."

"Dad?"

"Yes, Kyle?" Kyle was the larger and presumably older of the boys. He looked to be about eleven or twelve, Eddie perhaps a year younger.

"Can we ask Mr. Wilson what it's like to be in prison?"

"No," Keng said sharply. "You may not."

Wilson cleared his throat and said, "Uh, it isn't my place to contradict anything you tell your boys, but it's only natural they'd be curious. If they have questions it's all right with me. I'll answer them if I can. But that's if you say it's all right."

"All right! Can we, Pop, can we?" Kyle was practically jumping up and down. The contagion of the moment caught Eddie too, who quickly stepped up beside his brother and began pestering their father to open the door to questions. "We never met a real live convict before, Daddy. Can we, huh?"

Keng gave Lyle an apologetic look and said, "Are you sure you wouldn't mind?"

"I minded being there but there's no use pretending that it didn't happen, for it surely did. It's all right with me if the boys ask their questions."

Keng looked sternly down at his sons and said, "All right then. You can talk with Mr. Wilson after we have our dinner. Mind now, you'll wait until after. Then you can talk with him."

Kyle gave a loud whoop and started to race away.

"Hold it," his father barked. Kyle stopped in his tracks. "Put the food basket on the table yonder before you go charging off someplace."

"Yes, sir. C'mon, Eddie. Let's go tell the other fellows." Both boys took off at a run.

"Uh-oh," Liza Keng said. "I think you may have quite an audience, Mr. Wilson."

Lyle smiled sheepishly, then shrugged. "Nothing like getting it all over with at once, I suppose."

"I do hope you like fried chicken," Liza offered, changing the subject. "And pies. Mrs. Darlon makes the most wonderful gooseberry pies."

"Liza makes a magnificent dried-apple pie her own self," Keng put in.

"I do hope you're hungry," the lady said.

"Why, ma'am, I got so much hunger I had to drive my wagon down today just to carry it all."

"And you always tell nothing but the truth," Keng added. "Isn't that right?"

"Yes, sir, it's absolutely true and nothing but. Now where should I set these beans?"

CHAPTER THIRTY-NINE

Bradley Thom heard someone softly moaning. He forced his eyes open, overcoming the gum that had developed in the corners of his eyelids, and realized that the sounds were coming unbidden from his own dry throat. He felt like hell on a meat hook. Probably looked worse. For damn sure smelled. He levered one arm high, dropped his head and sniffed at his own armpit, then made a sour face.

He felt his chin and neck, confirming what he already knew. He needed a shave. It had been . . . he couldn't remember how long. Several days anyway. He had shaved . . . mm . . . Tuesday? And this was Sunday. He was pretty sure about that, because there was that dance last night, the usual Saturday-night affair. He remembered that. Remembered the first part of it anyway. Then there had been a card game. He knew he'd sat in on that. Drinking. Some of the fellows were generous with the liquor. He had . . . It got hazy after that.

Thom checked his pockets. Empty. His head hurt something awful. The taste in his mouth was vile. Lord, he must have had himself a good time. He barked out a short, bitter laugh. The abrupt movement sent a jolt of pain through his skull.

He had a crick in his neck and his back ached. It

took him a moment to realize that he was seated in the wooden swivel armchair in his office. Apparently that was where he had spent the night. A good portion of the day too, judging by the bright sunshine in the street beyond the window. He had not been home in . . . since the last time he shaved, he supposed. Tuesday. Sunday. He grunted. The woman better not start in on him, complaining about that. Or anything else. Not if she knew what was good for her.

Thom stood up. It took him three tries and he had to brace his hands on the top of his desk once he did struggle upright, but he did it all right. His stomach lurched and for a moment he thought he would have to puke. He looked down to spot the trash can just in case it was suddenly needed.

He was hungry but the thought of food made his stomach roil and rumble. He would be sick for sure if he tried to eat right now. Coffee would be good though. Or another small shot of rye just to settle his gut. Medicinal, so to speak.

He found his hat—it was on the floor—and managed to pick it up without losing his balance. His head felt a little better once the hat was in place. He went out into the street and turned down the block toward his favorite saloon.

Jolly's was open. Jolly's was always open, or so it seemed sometimes. A scrawny, pinch-faced, ever-unsmiling fellow named Harry was behind the bar. His welcome was a grunt and a nod.

"Whiskey," Thom told him. "A glass, not a shot."

"Fine." Harry had a glass in his hand but made no move to set it on the bar nor to pick up a bottle. "Show me your money, Brad."

"What did you say?"

"You heard me. Show me some money."

"Dammit, man, my credit's good."

"No, Brad. It isn't. The boss cut you off last night. You don't remember that? Well he did. And you were tapped out then. No more credit, the man says. Cash on the line from here on."

"Dammit, don't you know who I am?"

"Of course I do, Brad. You're the guy that's got no more credit here. You already owe . . . You want me to look up your markers and figure it out? You ready to pay off?"

"I don't have . . ." His voice trailed away. He snorted once and ran his right wrist under his nose. "I don't have . . ."

"Go home, Brad. You had a bad night. Go home. Get cleaned up. You'll feel better."

Home. No booze there. No fun either. Just a nagging damn woman and noisy damn kids. Couldn't even have the damn woman. It was too soon, she claimed. What use was a woman if a man couldn't use her? Damn her.

She'd just start in whining again. Wanting money from him. That's all she ever wanted from him. And him with a lousy town marshal's job that paid a lousy twenty bucks a month. Damn wet-behind-the-ears cowherd made that much. It was no wage for a grown man. Brad only took the job for the prestige. And as a stepping-stone to something a lot better. County sheriff maybe, or even higher. Maybe much higher. But now . . . now there was a woman nagging at him and kids spitting up on his shirts and no money and now not even a little drink to settle a man's stomach and make him feel a little better about things.

"Look, Harry, draw me a beer anyway. I mean, what's

a lousy nickel's worth gonna hurt after all the business
I done here."

The barman shrugged. "Sorry, Brad, but I got my
instructions. Boss was pretty clear. I can't give you
even a small . . . Aw, hell. I hate to see a man turned
away. But don't tell the boss I did this, you hear me?"
Harry reached for one of the mugs upended in a pyra-
mid behind the bar.

Just this one, Thom told himself. Just the one beer to
settle his stomach and quell the pounding in his head.
Then he'd go home to Sarah and the boys. His boys.
Proof that he could get the job done. Yeah. Just this
one.

He belched and leaned his elbows on the bar top.
Thinking. Thinking about the future. About the money
he would make once he had that bastard Wilson's
place for his own. Charlie Darlon was going to help
him see to it. Handle the paperwork to make it all legal
and proper. He and Charlie cooked it up one evening.
Brad could not understand exactly how it was supposed to be done. The good thing was that he did not
have to. Charlie would take care of all that for him. All
Brad had to do was to get Wilson off the place. Make
him *eager* to get out.

He could do that. He was sure that he could.

What's more, he was looking forward to getting
some payback from that son of a bitch Wilson. Bradley
Thom knew how to run an outfit like that. Be a gentleman rancher. Run some cows and move up in politics
and . . . who knows where from there. He smiled to
himself and grunted with satisfaction. He would have
money enough for a drink or two then.

He sighed. He did wish he could get a whiskey now
though.

CHAPTER FORTY

"This is wonderful chicken, ma'am," Wilson said, reaching for another thigh, his third. "Cooked just right. You surely do know how."

"I should. We raise them. When Bubba decided to retire, we thought about what we should do next."

"Bubba?" Wilson asked. "Who would that be now?"

Liza rocked backward a little, cupping her hands together in front of her face and laughing. "I'm sorry. I keep forgetting. Bubba is what they used to call Leonard when he was in the rangers. No one here would know him by that name though."

"Rangers?" Wilson was beginning to feel lost.

"I used to be in the Arizona Rangers, Lyle," Keng said. "We try to keep that to ourselves." He looked at his wife and, with a smile, shrugged. "Some of us sometimes forget that and blab out loud."

"But I am proud of you," Liza protested with a pout. "I'm proud of what you did."

"Thank you, but you'll make our guest nervous with a lot of talk about the rangers."

"Because I used to be in prison? Not really, Leonard. I haven't done anything wrong and I don't intend to. You'll not make me nervous in the least."

"Good. I'm glad to hear that, Lyle. Are these beans your own cooking? They're mighty good. But to get back to the original subject, yes, we raise most of the table fryers you'll find around here and about half the local egg production. I looked around for quite a while before I chose a breed of bird that I liked. They gain better than anything else, they're plumper and juicier and they lay pretty well too. You might consider chickens yourself if you ever want to give up on cattle."

"Oh, I've already decided on that, Leonard. When I was sent up, the judge allowed me a little time to settle my affairs. I sold pretty much everything including all my livestock and even my brand."

"You'll have to go over to the county seat to register a new one then."

Wilson shook his head. "Won't be needing one. Just the other day I bought a flock of sheep and goats off Anders Donovan. Do you know him?"

"No, I'm afraid not," Keng said.

"He's a good man. Selling off here and retiring to Texas to be near . . . a daughter, I believe he said. Anyway, I bought his entire flock and took on Luis Santiago to herd them."

"I know Luis. He's all right. Seems to know his trade."

Wilson nodded. "He'll work for me on shares. Should be good for both of us."

"It sounds like you're getting everything very much under control again, Lyle. I'm glad. Too many men come out of prison hardened and bitter. They think society owes them compensation for the time they were in, and they feel entitled to take whatever they please because of it."

"Not me," Wilson said. "All I want is to be left alone so I can go on with my life."

"Good. I tell you what, though. You might want to give some thought to chickens. There is more of a market than I can . . . No, let me be honest about that. There is more of a market than I care to satisfy. I just don't want to work myself to death. We have enough, and 'enough' really should be enough for any man. This way I have time to spend with Liza and with our boys. We have a good life here. Why don't you come over some time, Lyle, and see our setup. See how we handle the birds, how we raise their feed, all of that." The tall man winked. "I could probably talk Liza into cooking you a chicken dinner if you come."

"That much temptation hardly seems fair," Wilson said.

"Mr. Wilson, are you ready to tell us about being a convict, sir?"

Eddie was tugging at Lyle's shirtsleeve. Wilson turned to look behind him and discovered at least a dozen small boys, and several little girls too, gathered there looking eager and excited. They were going to talk with a real live convict.

"Excuse me," Wilson told the Kengs. "Looks like I have a promise t' keep." He turned back to the children. "Now then. What is it that you young'uns are wanting t' know?"

CHAPTER FORTY-ONE

By the time Lyle finished talking—and eating—the sun was sinking toward the horizon and there was a gathering chill in the air. "I should've worn a coat or at least brought one along," he told the elderly man who had been informing Lyle of all the things he should do to turn his life around. An admonition to read three chapters daily from the Old Testament and one in the New were only the start of his advice.

Lyle got the impression that Wade Dellison was a busybody. But a sad and lonely busybody. Lyle did not really mind the old man's nattering, and in fact barely heard the squeak and rumble of his speech.

"If you'll excuse me, sir, I need to start for home," Lyle said, standing and arching his back to stretch tight muscles there.

"Next week. We can talk some more next week?" The inflection of his voice made the sentence more a question than a comment.

Lyle smiled. "Yes, sir. I'll look forward to visiting with you again next week." He helped Dellison climb creakily to his feet, then walked over to the table where the pans and baskets and many-hued bowls of food had been laid out for the picnic. The table was nearly empty now save for the stains and crumbs that the magpies and jays would soon flutter down to finish off.

Wilson collected his bean pot and was pleased to note that only a few greasy smears remained in it. Apparently his effort had been enjoyed. So had the towel he had used as a hot pad. The towel had disappeared. He stifled his inclination to cuss whoever took the nearly new towel and sighed instead. Damn them though, he grumbled in silence. Damn them all to hell and gone.

Pastor Moore and Eva were on the church steps, in deep conversation with a young family there. Lyle waved but did not think they saw, as neither of them responded.

He went to his wagon and set the bean pot on the floor beneath his seat, then walked forward to the mare's head. Some time during the afternoon she had managed to spit the bit out of her mouth. It dangled now under her chin, still attached to the lead of the hitch weight but no longer doing any good to hold her in place.

"It's a good thing you ain't spooky," Lyle mumbled as he unclipped the weight and put it into the wagon beside the bean pot. Then he returned to the mare's head, held her jaw with one hand while he maneuvered the bit back into her mouth with the other. "If this keeps up, little lady, I'll have to adjust the headstall so it sets higher in your mouth. Maybe even buy a spade bit. That'd show you. You might not like that so good. So quit your messing around and act nice." While he was chiding the mare with words she could not understand, he was scratching the hollow beneath her jaw in the spot that she liked best. Unlike the words, and quite the opposite of them, she could understand that perfectly well.

Only two other rigs, one open buggy and a closed

opera coach, remained in the church lot, so Lyle did not have to back his wagon out. He simply turned the mare's head and clucked her into motion, wheeling around in a tight turn that took them out onto the road.

"All right, old girl, let's have a trot an' take us home, if you please."

His mood was good. The evening was clear and lovely, with stars beginning to flicker in and out of view in the darkening sky. Lyle cleared his throat, looked around to make sure there was no one else on the road on a Sunday eve, and began to sing. Loudly, if not well.

He never saw the attackers until they were already on him.

CHAPTER FORTY-TWO

The mare seemed familiar enough with the way back to her evening feeding, and some time in the past mile or two Lyle had quieted his singing and dropped into a light doze, his upper body swaying and softly bumping with the travel of the unsprung wagon, chin tucked and arms crossed over his chest.

He roused at the scuff of boot leather on hard ground. Felt a momentary panic at his disorientation as he woke, in that instant reacting as if he were on his cot back in the prison cell and a crowd of bullying inmates were swarming over him.

Wilson lashed out, his fist contacting hard muscle. He heard a grunt of pain and a curse.

The wagon tilted to the other side as a second highwayman climbed on behind Lyle's back while he was trying to fight off the first.

Two of them then. At least.

He felt a blow across his shoulders and upper back. Something hard and slender. A chunk of wood, perhaps, or an ax handle. The implement glanced off the side of his head when it landed. His hat fell spinning to the floor of the wagon and his right ear stung, the feeling almost like it had been burned.

Lyle gave the shadowy figure in front of him a hard shove, sending him backward and dumping him on the ground. He whirled, an elbow crunching into flesh.

That man withdrew with a short cry of pain.

Wilson yanked the driving lines and brought the mare to a halt. He jumped down to the ground and went on the offensive, ignoring the fellow on the far side of the rig and attacking the one who was wielding the club.

Wilson's vision was blurred and he could barely see anyway in the new-fallen darkness, but he charged blindly forward, fists flailing and feet flying too.

"Hey!" the half-seen figure barked, indignation thick in his voice as if he thought Wilson was not fighting fair.

Wilson kicked him again. The man turned and scampered out of reach of Wilson's hard kicks.

"C'mon. Let's get t' hell outa here."

Wilson was certain he had heard that voice before. "Bannerman? Is that you, you son of a bitch?"

He heard footsteps behind him again. Hart? Almost certainly. Bannerman and Hart—one was rarely seen without the other.

Before Wilson could turn to meet Thomas Hart, he was hit low in the back and catapulted forward off his feet.

He hit the ground facedown. Felt the stab of a boot toe drive into his left hip.

Lyle Wilson had been in similar circumstances before. He curled into a tight ball, arms wrapped over his head and knees drawn up toward his chest.

The kicks rained down, swiftly at first, then slower and more deliberate as the two began to tire.

Wilson had no idea how long it went on before he finally found a measure of relief in unconsciousness.

CHAPTER FORTY-THREE

"Mister. Mister, are you all right?"

Wilson came back to consciousness all at once. And was immediately sorry that he had done so.

He hurt. Everywhere. He hurt deep and hard and ugly. Ribs, arms, the small of his back. His head. Lordy, his head. It felt like a pumpkin that dropped off the back of a wagon. Surely it must have been split wide, wide open in order to hurt so bad. But he was alive. That was the good news. He was alive.

"Mister?"

It took Wilson some effort but he managed to get his eyes open. He could see a shadowy form looming over him. It was only then that he realized that he was lying down. He had no idea how he had come to do so. Or where he was. He moved a little. Felt dirt and stones and grit. He was lying on the ground, then. He groaned.

"Well, you're alive," the voice above him said. "Reckon that's something. How bad you hurt, mister? Can you get up? D'you need help? Now that was a dumb question, wa'n't it. O' course you need help. Come on then. Lemme get you up. Put you in the coach. I'll take you in t' town. See can we find somebody awake at this hour. Somebody t' take care of you."

Wilson felt strong hands slip under his armpits and

lift. He tried to help but his benefactor had to take nearly all of Wilson's weight on himself.

The man pulled Wilson into a sitting position, moved around behind him to get a better lift and hauled him upright and then forward. He mumbled while he lifted. "You're one lucky son of a bitch," the fellow said. "I wouldn't a' seen you myself, come to that I didn't see you, woulda drove right over top of you, but my leaders seen you. Boogered something awful. It's lucky they didn't get over the traces or tip the coach over or somethin'. It was them as seen you, don't you see. So I stopped. O' course I did. That's the only reason I found you was them horses. See if you can help me a little here. See if you can stay on your feet while I get this door open. Lean up agin the side o' the coach for just a minute. Can you do that for me, mister?"

Wilson heard a metallic click. That would be the door latch, he supposed. He felt himself being pushed forward onto the floor of a coach. Every slight movement of joint or muscle brought waves of pain and spasms from protesting flesh. He hurt . . . everywhere.

The man—the stagecoach driver—climbed over top of him to get inside the vehicle, then reached down and pulled. Wilson managed to get his legs working just a little to help. He tumbled forward and the driver crawled over him again, this time to get out of the coach.

Wilson wound up lying halfway inside the coach with his lower half still hanging out. He was bent double with his nose pressed hard into the gritty, soiled carpet on the floor between the seats. The carpet smelled terrible. Wilson clenched his mouth tight shut lest he taste some of the leavings of countless boots.

"There now, that's better. We'll pull this robe over

top of you. Keep you warm till we can find you some help in Fox Hill, which in case you don't know is the next town up the line. You got to pull your legs up a little if you can. Your feet is sticking out an' I can't close the door."

Wilson felt his feet being pushed, his legs bending.

"There, that's better. All right. It won't be long. We're only a couple miles out o' town if I remember correct. Don't go nowhere now."

Wilson heard a faint chuckle and then the sound of the coach door closing and the latch snapping shut. A moment later the coach sagged down a little on one side as the driver climbed back up onto the box.

He heard a shrill whistle and a horse's snort, and then the coach lurched forward.

Wilson closed his eyes and let the welcome blackness come over him once again.

CHAPTER FORTY-FOUR

"Now, they's been a crime committed, Marshal, an' in your capacity as the deppity sherf for this end o' the county it's gonna be up t' you to investigate it. You hear what I'm tellin' you, Brad? You're gonna want t' make a show of investigatin' this here crime, but you might want t' keep in mind that we done it for you as much as for us." Tom Hart giggled. "Well, almost as much as for us."

"What did you do? And how much did you get?" Bradley Thom demanded.

"We were out east of town, sitting there in the scrub minding our own business," Willy Bannerman said, "when that felon Lyle Wilson came driving by. We know he's no favorite of yours so we sort of, well, we sort of jumped him. Beat him up."

"We mostly done it for you," Hart put in. "We know that's the sorta thing you'd want done anyhow, so when we seen that good a chance, well, we took it."

"Damned thoughtful of both of you, I'm sure," Thom said, his voice dry and expression hard. "So how much did he have on him?"

" 'Bout seventy dollars," Hart said.

"Seventy two and a quarter," Bannerman corrected. "We figure your share comes to seven and a quarter."

"Make it an even ten," the Fox Hill town marshal

said. "That's so much easier than trying to work out fractions." He chuckled. "Friendlier too."

"Dammit, Brad, I—" Bannerman stopped before his protest went too far to back away from. He turned to Hart. "Give him a eagle, Tommy."

Hart dutifully fished a gold eagle out of his pocket and handed it to the marshal.

"Thanks. So tell me, did you kill the son of a bitch?"

"Dunno if he's died or not. He was still breathing when we left." Hart turned to his partner and asked, "Don't you agree, Willy?"

Bannerman shrugged. "We didn't get down on the ground with him to see. He might still be alive. We beat him pretty good though. D'you want us to go back and make sure he's dead? We'd do that for you, Brad."

"Cheap," Hart said.

"It wouldn't be a bad thing if the man was to die," Thom mused aloud. "But I don't want it bad enough to pay for it. Besides, I don't have any money. Not to speak of, I don't."

"We'd go back an' finish him off for that ten-piece you got in your hand there," Hart offered. He grinned. "That's a real bargain rate, you got to admit."

"Thanks, but I'm needing this tenner. My old woman's been bitching something awful. Says she needs shit for the kids." Thom shrugged. "No sale."

"Yeah, well, if you ever do want the man done, you just let us know. We don't like him much better than you do."

Thom stood and began extinguishing the lamps that burned in the town marshal's office. "I'd best get along now," he said as he herded his visitors toward the door. "Don't you boys worry yourselves about this crime spree in town. I'll search for the bandits, but somehow I doubt that I'll catch them." He winked, then blew out the last lamp. "See you fellas tomorrow, eh?"

"G'night, Brad."

"Good night now."

The marshal carefully locked the door behind him and checked that the latch had caught, then walked out into the dark, empty street as he headed for home.

CHAPTER FORTY-FIVE

It was the motionlessness that roused him after the sway and jolt of being on the stagecoach floor. He suspected he had been away for a while though. Unconscious, not sleeping. Sleep would have been welcome. So would a cessation of the pain that racked his body from top to bottom.

He came aware now that the coach quit moving and he wondered about that. He would have thought it would be the other way around, that he would be able to sleep when the outfit was still but would be awakened when it moved.

And why, he wondered, was he thinking about inconsequential things like that when he should be thinking about . . . what? Just what the hell should he be thinking about now?

All he knew right now, dammit, was that he hurt. Lordy, but he did hurt. His head felt like someone had taken an ax to it—come to think of it, maybe they had—and his eyes were swollen shut so that he could not see a thing. He tried to open them and look around but could not.

He could still taste things. Bile and grit and blood.

And he could hear. He heard the creak of leather springs and a faint jangle of chains. The movement of the coach body settling down on one side and then back up again made him want to puke. The sour acid stink on the coach floor close beside his head suggested that he already lost most of what he had eaten at the church picnic that day.

That day. Had it been so recent? It felt like that pleasant afternoon was many days past.

He heard voices. Distant. Or at least dim. Voices. The squeal and slap of a spring-loaded gate being opened and then snapping closed.

Grind of gravel underfoot. More than one set of boots? He thought so.

Click of the coach door latch.

"Are you sure you want him?" Wilson thought that was the driver's voice. He seemed to remember it from when he was picked up.

"Uh-huh." He could not tell who that would be.

Someone reached in and pulled on his ankles, straightening his legs so that once again he was only partially inside.

"Can you get him?"

"Uh-huh."

"Here, let me help. Can you move aside? Just a little. There. Now, pull." Wilson felt himself sliding. Someone was pulling his legs. "Careful now. Don't drop him." A chuckle. "Not that I think you'd do any more damage than's already been done." There was a pause, then, "Take his feet. I'll get him under the arms. Damn!"

"What's wrong?"

"D'you see what the son of a bitch done in my coach? I'm gonna have t' throw that piece o' rug away. Even if I could clean it it'd still stink."

"Look out. He's falling."

"No, he ain't. I got him. But I ain't happy with him right now."

"I appreciate you bringing him," the other voice said. Wilson was sure he had heard it before but he could not place it.

"Didn't see that I had much choice," the driver said. "Not short of dumping him out in the street, I didn't. Idiot kid over at the telegraph office said they didn't want him there. Saw who it was an' said he didn't want no criminal there. Said the prison rat didn't deserve no human kindness. Now me, I always figure a man should be treated decent. That's why I thought o' you."

"You did the right thing. Get him . . . watch your step going up."

The sound of gravel changed to the sound of feet on wood. There was the screech of a door spring and a new scent in the air. Flowery. Nice.

Wilson felt himself being shifted around in another direction. He could tell because there were lights. At least two lamps. They swung around. Or rather he swung around in relation to them.

"Here. On the sofa. Be careful now." A woman's voice. He thought he had heard that one too. He tried again to open his eyes but they were swollen shut.

The driver and this new benefactor placed him carefully down onto something soft—a sofa, the woman's voice mentioned a sofa—and a little too short for him, so his feet hung off to the side.

"That should do. Thanks."

"Sure. Any time, padre."

"Get some water, Evan," the girl said. Evan, she had said. So she would be Eva Moore and he would be in the preacher's house now. "Warm. Mix some hot from the reservoir with some cold from the jug. And bring a cloth. I need to clean him up. At the very least I need to wash some of that dried blood away so we can see where he has been hurt."

"Do we have anything we can use for bandages?"

"I'll find something. Now go on, please. Get that warm water."

"I won't be a minute."

Wilson felt a hand—soft, warm—very lightly touch his forehead, then his cheek.

It seemed very silly under the circumstances, but he felt the same physical responses to Eva Moore as he had before, and this time there was nothing he could do to hide it. The best he could hope for was that she did not see.

His problem resolved itself when he passed out of consciousness again.

CHAPTER FORTY-SIX

Wilson returned to a world filled with pain and suffering. He hurt from the soles of his feet to the top of his head. Actually, he realized, that was something of an exaggeration. The top of his head did indeed hurt but the bottoms of his feet were unscathed. That might have been the only part of him that had not been kicked, pummeled and pounded on . . . but only because of the thick sole leather that protected the bottoms of his feet. Otherwise he was sure those would be in pain right now too.

"Are you all right?" It was a woman's voice, so probably it was Eva Moore who was at his side.

Wilson wanted to shout "Hell, no," but he did not. Pain is something best kept to oneself. That was a lesson he had learned long ago. He struggled to open his eyes. They felt like they were glued closed.

"Here. Let me help." Her voice was gentle. So was her touch. He felt the press of a warm, wet cloth over his eyes, then his forehead and cheeks. It made him feel like a little boy again, when his mother used to wash his face like that in the mornings. He had not thought about that in years but it came rushing back now.

He managed to open his eyes. Blinked rapidly several times. Instead of the rough-hewn timber walls of his barely remembered boyhood home, however, he saw the thoroughly modern interior of the manse. Saw the preacher's wife seated on a chair that had been moved around so that it—and she—sat now beside the sofa where he lay.

She was lovely. Her cheeks were flushed a light red. The color went nicely with her complexion. With that clear, smooth, soft flesh of her face and arms and . . . she was wearing a loose housedress, and when she bent forward to lave his face with the warm water, he could not help but see . . . more than she would have liked anyone other than her husband to see.

Wilson rolled his head the other way. Too late to avoid the physical response to Eva, but he tried. Surely he should get credit for that. He turned his head away when what he wanted, what he ached to do instead, was not only to look beneath Eva's clothing but to touch her as well. He wanted to touch what he had seen. Wanted to press his face to her softness and kiss her. Smell her. Taste her.

He did no such thing, and his embarrassment removed the problem in his britches almost as quickly as it had come upon him.

He realized there was something wrong with the image he saw when he turned his head that way, and it took him a moment to recognize the problem. On that side of the room he could see the Moores' sofa placed against the wall. He remembered being on it. Remembered that his feet hung off the side because it was too short to lie upon full length. Yet now he was stretched flat and his feet and lower legs were supported.

So where . . . ? Ah. He saw the strips of raw wood and an edge of hard canvas and realized they had brought in a folding camp cot and placed him on that.

With some sort of mattress too. Straw? Probably. Whatever, it was . . . not exactly comfortable. His injuries prevented that. But he was less miserable than he might have been.

"Hello," Eva said. She was smiling. Lordy, but she was a handsome young woman when she smiled. "You're back."

His brow furrowed. He did not recall having gone anywhere.

"Do you know how long you've been here?" She paused a moment to dip her rag into a basin that she held in her lap, then squeezed some of the water out of the cloth and leaned forward to again bathe his face. And his torso as well.

He felt another flush of embarrassment, quite acute this time, as he recognized for the first time that he was naked. He seemed to be covered by a blanket that had been pushed down to his waist, but underneath that blanket he was naked. He hoped he at least still had his drawers on.

"This is the fifth day," Eva said as she washed his chest and upper arms, dampened the cloth and washed his face again. "We were becoming worried about you. We thought . . ." She pinched her lips together and shook her head, declining to say what they might have thought. "You must be hungry. Would you like something to eat? I have some chicken broth simmering for you nice and hot. The Kengs sent over some birds so we could keep you supplied. That was nice of them, don't you think? They are good people. Understanding."

Eva dropped the cloth into her basin and stood. "I'll bring your broth first. Then I'll go find Marshal Thom and tell him you've wakened. I know he will want to know. And Evan, of course. He will want to pray with you after Marshal Thom pries at you. I won't be a moment."

She turned, her skirts flaring, and hustled away, leaving her scent behind. Wilson tried to struggle upright. He strained and bit his lip to keep from crying out in response to the pain his movement caused.

He wanted to sit up. Wanted to find his clothing. Stand. Get the hell out of there before Mrs. Moore came back and he had to face the embarrassment of knowing that she must have seen him naked.

He could not move. His muscles simply would not respond that well. And the pain became even worse.

Yet in his mind's eye the image remained of what he had been able to see down the front of Mrs. Moore's housedress.

CHAPTER FORTY-SEVEN

Bradley Thom's glowering presence seemed to fill the room. The man seemed huge, but Wilson recognized quickly enough that this could be at least partially explained by the fact that he himself was lying flat on his cot while Thom stood over him. And the man was also standing beside little Evan Moore. Lyle felt tall when he stood beside Evan. When he could stand at all, that is.

"Tell me about it," Thom demanded without preamble. He did not bother with any sort of greeting or sympathy. Not that Lyle would have believed him had either been offered.

Lyle shrugged. The gesture hurt but he did it without thinking about that consequence. He had been beaten in prison but never this badly. And that had been a long time ago. The other inmates learned soon enough to leave him alone. For two reasons. One was that no amount of beating seemed to change Lyle Wilson's mind about anything. The other was that as soon as he was sufficiently healed he would look to take revenge on anyone who attacked him. He also learned to defend himself so that it became more and more difficult to get to him. The others learned that it was simply more sensible to leave Wilson alone.

"How many were there?" Thom asked, his voice

harsh as if he did not believe Wilson had been attacked at all but might have done this to himself for some obscure purpose.

"I . . ." Wilson cleared his throat. Licked dry lips. His voice sounded like someone had shoved a rasp down his throat. He took a deep, slow breath and then tried again. "I don't know. It was dark. They came at me from behind. I never got a good look at them."

"Them, you say. There was more than one?"

Wilson nodded. "Aye, I'm sure of that much. I handled the first one. Then another, maybe several more, jumped me from behind. So there was at least two. Could've been more. I just don't know."

"You might like to know that I started looking for them as soon as I heard about this. We've never been friends, you and me, but it's my sworn duty to bring down anyone that would jump an hones—" Thom stopped for a moment and reconsidered what he had been about to say. "I'll bring down anyone who commits a crime in this town or within my jurisdiction as a deputy sheriff regardless of who or what their victim is. Even if the victim is a jailbird like you, Wilson."

"Be careful what you say, Bradley," Evan Moore said, getting into the conversation for the first time. Lyle had almost forgotten that the little preacher was there. "Lyle is a guest in my home. An injured traveler at that." He looked up at Thom and added, "You don't want me to speak on the subject of those who passed by the wounded traveler, do you? The traveler who was given succor by the Good Samaritan?"

"I didn't mean nothing, preacher. Like I was saying to this miserable son of a bi— Excuse me, Miss Moore, I didn't see you standing there. Like I was saying to Wilson, there's a crime been done. It's my job to catch

the ones as done it. If I can find out who that would
be . . . a pack o' youngsters maybe, out on a prowl . . .
I'll sure enough bring them in an' charge them. But so
far I got no leads to who it might've been."

"Fine, Bradley. I'm sure you will do your best," Evan
said.

"What about you, Wilson? Can you add anything to
the little that I know?" Thom asked.

"No. I reckon I can't." You don't peach to the guards
when you're inside and you don't complain to the law
outside either.

"All right then." To Moore, Marshal Thom said, "If
you hear of anything, you let me know, Preacher. An'
if you need me for anything, like if he dies or something, you know where to find me."

"He is not going to die, Bradley. And yes, I know
where to find you."

"All right then." Thom nodded in the direction of
the doorway into the kitchen, put his hat back on and
turned to go.

Evan saw the marshal out and followed him onto
the front porch while Eva came out of the kitchen to
cluck over Wilson and try to make him more comfortable. "Bradley will find whoever did this," she said in
a soft, soothing voice.

Lyle snorted and managed a grin. "Dear lady, that
ol' boy not only won't find them, he won't even look.
The only reason he came here was to show off to your
brother, lest Evan say things against him in town.
Evan could bring Brad down in a heartbeat, and Brad
knows it. Him and me, we been on opposite sides of
things for a long time. Me going to prison only added
to that, it didn't start it."

"If you say so." She sounded like she did not believe

it but did not pursue the matter. "So tell me. Are you hungry for something more substantial than broth? I have some chicken and dumplings on the stove. They will be ready soon."

The thought of solid food made Lyle's stomach lurch and gurgle. Hungry? He was damn near starved. But all he said aloud was a polite, "Yes, ma'am. I could stand to eat."

CHAPTER FORTY-EIGHT

Bradley Thom sat at his kitchen table, wide awake despite the predawn dark outside. Five o'clock, he guessed, or thereabouts. Early, anyway. He picked up his coffee cup and, holding it in both hands, breathed in the aroma for a moment before he very delicately took a careful sip. He liked his coffee hot—like his women, he used to say—but did not care for the feeling when he burned his lip or tongue.

Thom looked across to the far side of the kitchen to where Sarah was standing over the stove with a wooden spatula. He scowled at what he saw. Sarah was not the slim and sexy little number he had married three years ago. Then, she was always clean and tidy. Now, after bearing two children, her butt had begun to spread and her bosoms sagged. This morning her hair was unkempt and she was barefoot, her legs splayed wide like she was some damned Mex woman waddling back and forth.

She wore a housecoat that she had not bothered to tie closed, and looking at her from behind, Brad doubted his wisdom in choosing her. Still, her family was well regarded in the county. Old Jim Hanson could help pull in a good many votes. And Bradley Thom wanted much more for himself than to be a mere town marshal.

At this point he figured he could handle the town vote on his own. He no longer needed Jim for that. But his ambitions ran far outside of Fox Hill, and out in the county Jim had much more influence than Brad did.

Bradley Thom thought he would be an ideal sheriff. Now there was an office with a world of opportunity for the collection of fees. Or county judge. Perhaps someday a territorial office. Why, a presidential appointment as governor was not out of the realm of possibility. Not if he played his cards right. And he did intend to play his cards right.

"Sarah."

She turned, eyes downcast, expression carefully neutral. "Yes, Bradley?"

" 'Bout last night. That wasn't me. That was just the whiskey. You know I wouldn't never hurt you nor the boys, either one. I wouldn't do that. It was just the whiskey."

"Yes, Bradley. It was the whiskey, that's all."

"Come here to me."

Sarah shuffled barefoot across the linoleum floor of their little house on Third. She stopped in front of him and stood there, without allowing her eyes to meet his. "Yes, Bradley?"

He said nothing for a time, letting her stand mute while he inspected her. There were no bruises on her face—he'd learned about that a long while back—but he was concerned there might be marks on her neck. He seemed to recall grabbing her by the throat, so he tugged the neck of her nightgown down. There were some marks high on her chest. Those might have been old, but that did not matter. "If you go out today I want you to wear a dress with a high neck. Right up high on your throat. That blue dress, maybe. You know the one I mean?"

"Yes, of course."

"You wear that today. And let me see your arms."

Sarah peeled her sleeves back, first one and then the other. She presented her arms and wrists for her husband's inspection. There were bruises, but they were all high on her forearms. Brad grunted and nodded, and Sarah allowed her sleeves to fall back where they had been.

"Is there anything else you want to see, Bradley?"

He was not sure if she might be twisting his tail with that comment. She might be. She knew well enough that he went with whores. She used to blame herself for that and tried to find ways to please him so that he would keep it at home. Eventually she gave up. If she cared any longer she was silent about it. Usually. Once in a while she would let off accumulated steam, but not often.

"No. Go on back to your cooking, woman. I don't want you to burn my breakfast."

"It's ready now."

"Then serve it, damn you. Don't be keeping me waiting." Quick anger surged up within him and for a moment, sober or not, he wanted to hit her again. He forced the anger back and picked up the coffee cup.

"Yes, Bradley." Sarah used her apron to protect her hands from the hot metal as she moved both of her skillets to the side of the stove surface. She took a clean plate down from the cabinet and used her spatula to scoop a flat of fry bread onto it, then carried both the plate and the smaller skillet to the table. She set them down for her husband and took a half step back. She stood still until he nodded to dismiss her.

Sarah returned to her stove to finish making the fry

bread that she would give to Bradley Junior when he woke up. Little Bryan was beginning to take a little soft food but he was mostly still at the breast.

Brad looked at his wife standing at the stove, looked without really seeing. He grunted once and squared his shoulders, trying to force his thoughts back to the here and now. He tore off a bit of fry bread and wallowed it around in the grease that pooled in the skillet beside him, then popped the dripping bite into his mouth and chewed. Fry bread and bacon grease. It didn't get much better than that.

Brad was thinking about higher office—which he should reach for and when—while he absently picked up a thick slice of fried jowl and bit off a generous chunk of the fatty meat.

Sheriff next, he pondered? No, it would be sensible to shore up his Fox Hill base first. Justice of the peace next, Brad thought. Then county sheriff. County judge. Perhaps United States marshal after that. And . . . who knows? . . . territorial governor. It was a line of thought that was perhaps Bradley's very favorite. He swallowed the bite of jowl and took another sip of coffee.

Life, he thought, was good.

CHAPTER FORTY-NINE

"You have a visitor," Eva rather proudly told Wilson after peering out the front window toward what little traffic there was on the street. A moment later Lyle heard the gate and then saw the top of a man's hat pass by a side window. Whoever it was seemed to be comfortable enough to go around to the back without first announcing himself.

Eva made a quick circuit around the parlor, tugging and plumping and straightening. She shifted Lyle's feet on the footstool—not that he particularly wanted them moved—and smoothed the lap robe that covered him. He was sitting up in an armchair now. It was something of an accomplishment.

Several minutes passed; then the brown hat went by in the other direction. Lyle heard footsteps on the porch. Eva waited until she heard a polite rap on the front door before she went to greet the guest.

Lyle was more or less expecting the person to be Jim Hanson or Luis Santiago, with an outside chance that it could be Sam Arnold. Instead it was tall, rangy, smiling Leonard Keng who first wiped his feet, then removed his hat and stepped inside.

Keng greeted Eva and said, "I brought four chickens. Put 'em around back in the cage."

"Thank you, Leonard. Would you like to see Lyle?"

"Of course. I couldn't come calling on you, Eva. Not in broad daylight anyway." He winked. "I'm a married man."

"Happily, I hope," she shot back at him.

"Indeed so." Keng turned his attention across the room to where Lyle was propped up in Evan's easy chair, buried to the eyeballs in blankets and robes. "You," Keng said with a pointing finger and an accusing voice. "You were supposed to come to our house for dinner last week. Instead you were sleeping."

"I'm—I'm sorry, Mr. Keng, I . . ."

Keng laughed and strode across the room with his hand extended to shake. "Good Lord, Wilson, I'm tugging your leg. We'd already heard about you being attacked. We knew where you were. And why. No harm was done and certainly no apologies are in order."

"You and your family are very kind, Mr. Keng."

"Leonard," he said. "Please call me Leonard." He laughed. "Better yet, call me what my friends do. That's Bubba."

"All right. Bubba."

"Can I get you anything, Leonard?" Eva asked, hovering between them. "Tea? Milk? Anything at all?"

"No, nothing for me, thanks."

"Lyle?"

He shook his head.

"Then I shall leave you two to plot your villainy and—" She stopped. Abruptly. And looked embarrassed. Obviously she had just remembered that Lyle had indeed been convicted of a certain amount of villainy. "Well, um . . . I have things I need to do." She twisted her hands in her apron, uncertain what to do with them.

"Don't forget those birds," Keng said. "I didn't give them any feed or water."

"Yes. Thank you." Eva dropped her by-now-rather-abused apron and hurried toward the back of the house.

Keng dragged a chair near and sat, leaning forward with his forearms resting on his knees. "How are you doing, Lyle?"

"Upright. A little. That's an improvement."

"If it helps to relieve your worries, when I heard what happened to you I rode over to your place. Your mare was standing outside the corral gate waiting for someone to let her in. I took the liberty of bringing her back to my place so we could take care of her while you're laid up. I didn't see any other livestock."

"I, uh, come to think of it, I did buy some. But they're being taken care of." He took another long look at the chicken farmer and said, "You're the walking, talking model for that stuff they call Christian charity, aren't you?"

Keng laughed. "I'm only being a neighbor."

"A helluva lot more than that, if you will excuse the expression. Anyway, thank you. I can't tell you how much I appreciate . . ." He started to feel a most unexpected flood of emotion well up in the back of his throat and in his eyes. "I appreciate . . . Sorry." Lyle pulled the neck of his borrowed nightshirt high and used it to wipe his eyes. "Sorry."

"Not to change the subject or anything, but how are you and Miss Eva getting along?" Keng laughed again. "You know, Lyle, if the men of this town already suspect you because of your past, now they're probably close to hating you because you're spending so much time here with that lovely girl. She has every bachelor in Fox Hill sniffing around her."

Lyle gave the man a questioning look. "Why would they do that? She's married, right?"

Keng's laughter rang loud this time. "Good Lord, man. You've been thinking that . . . Oh, that's rich." He slapped his knee and rocked back in his chair a little. "Evan and Eva aren't man and wife, Lyle. They're brother and sister."

"I'll be damned," Lyle blurted.

"Could be," Keng said pleasantly, "but that's not for you or me to say. Now then, is there anything I can do for you? Loan you a book, perhaps? Bring you a checkers board? Anything?"

"I'm sure I'll think of a dozen things you could do for me, Bubba. They'll likely come to me right after you leave."

"Then if there is nothing right now, Lyle"—the former ranger leaned forward again—"tell me how you got here. Every little detail you can recall."

CHAPTER FIFTY

"Such a nice man," Eva said after escorting Keng to the door on his way home. She stood by Lyle's chair and looked down at him for a moment, then said, "Is there anything I can get you?" After several long moments of silence she added, "Is something wrong? Did Leonard say something to you? Why are you looking at me like that?"

"I . . ." He shook his head. "Nothing's wrong. And I don't need anything right now, thanks."

Nothing might be wrong, but something had certainly changed. He saw Eva in a much different light now. She was a single girl, not a married woman. And she was even prettier than before. If that were possible.

"Lyle! Are you all right? Why is your face flushed? Do you have a fever?"

Flushed? he thought. No, that was not it at all. And he had no fever.

Eva came closer, squatted down beside him and pressed the back of her hand and then her palm against his cheeks and forehead, trying to gauge his temperature from that.

Except he had no fever. He was blushing rather than flushed. He could feel the heat in his face when he remembered that this girl, this unmarried girl, must have been the one to bathe and clean him up after he was brought into her home like a bird with a broken wing, thrown there for the preacher and his family to care for.

And the thoughts flooded over him. The thoughts about Eva that he had so carefully been keeping bottled up. Until now. Until now that he knew she was single and available and . . . so lovely. Small and delicate and lovely.

Lyle blinked and looked away, trying once more to not think about her that way.

"Lyle? I asked you if you are all right."

"I'm . . . fine. Just fine, Miss Moore."

"Miss? I thought we had gotten past that, Mr. Wilson. I presume you do want me to call you Mister now. Or would you prefer that I call you by all three of your names from now on? Come to think of it, Mr. Wilson, I don't know all three of your names. So what is your middle name? Unless it's secret. Will you refuse to tell me?"

He could think of nothing that he would refuse her. Not that he could exactly tell her that. But he certainly felt it. "It's, um, not a secret," he admitted.

"Then what is it?"

"Actually, uh, truth is that Lyle is my middle name. The full version is Christopher Lyle Wilson. But I've been called Lyle all my life, pretty much. I don't know why."

"Christopher Lyle," she repeated slowly. Then Eva nodded. "It's nice. I like it."

"But please. Just call me Lyle, Miss Moore."

Her laughter sounded like tiny bells ringing. "But you call me Miss? Now why should that be, Mr. Moore?"

"I, well, I just found out that you aren't . . . that is,

that you are . . ." He sighed. "Never mind. It was just a misunderstanding."

Eva chuckled and shook her pretty head. "I do declare, Mr. Moore, that I shall never, not as long as I live, I shall never understand men. Now if you will excuse me, sir, I need to go tend to those chickens Leonard brought."

Eva left the room but her scent lingered, and as soon as she was well clear of the door and could not see, Lyle leaned forward and breathed in the air where the girl had just stood.

Funny thing though. Now that he knew, he felt strange, perhaps even a little uncomfortable, staying in this home where Eva Moore and her brother lived.

Lyle sat back in the comfortable armchair, closed his eyes and tried to avoid thinking about the things he most wanted to think of.

CHAPTER FIFTY-ONE

"I can't tell you how much . . . how much I appreciate what the two of you have done for me. You saved my life. Truly you did." Wilson stood in the doorway of the manse, half in and halfway out of the house that had been his home for more than two weeks.

"We did nothing but our Christian duty," Evan Moore said.

"You went the extra mile," Wilson insisted, "and I'll be forever grateful to both of you."

Eva smiled up at him and offered her hand. He touched it as gingerly as if it were a rare and fragile flower. He did not look into the pretty girl's eyes when he did so. But then he had not once made eye contact with her in the days since he learned she was the pastor's sister and not his wife.

"Are you ready, Lyle?"

"Yes, sir," he said over his shoulder to Leonard Keng, who was standing on the porch waiting to drive Wilson home.

Wilson shook hands with Moore, hesitated and then gave the preacher a bear hug. "I'll never be able to thank you enough," he said. He turned to Keng and accepted the bigger man's assistance down the porch steps and out to the buggy. Wilson's mare was tied on behind.

"She looks fat and sassy," he said, nodding toward the bay.

Keng helped Wilson up into the buggy seat and offered a robe for him to spread over his lap. "She probably is pretty sassy at that. Hasn't done a lick of work in more than two weeks and she looks like she has some spirit in her. Should be she'll get some of that walked out of her on the drive down to your place."

"What about my wagon?" Lyle asked. He was afraid the vehicle might have been damaged when the mare dragged it home without him after he was attacked on the road.

"It's fine. I left it sitting in the yard there. I hope that's all right."

"Of course. I was just worried what might've happened to it, the mare taking it home on her own like that."

"There was no damage that I could see. Do you have any better idea who it was that jumped you like that?" Keng picked up the driving lines in one hand and the buggy whip in the other. Wilson turned and waved to the Moores, who were standing on the front porch to see him off.

With a snap of the whip popper and a shake of the lines, the light buggy rolled forward.

Wilson swiveled around in the seat so he could look back for the last possible glimpse of Eva Moore. Leonard Keng glanced toward him, then softly chuckled. "Git up, old son," Keng said with another pop of the whip. "Get along there."

CHAPTER FIFTY-TWO

"Would you like me to come in with you and help get you settled?"

"Thank you, but I can manage." Lyle grinned. "I better be able to."

"All right. If you think you can. I'll turn the mare in to the corral. There's hay in the bunk and all the water she could want, and I grained her this morning before I left the house, so she'll be all right for a spell. Oh, and before I forget, your harness is hanging over there in the shed. I put it under cover in case it rained or we had a heavy dew while you were laid up."

"I can't begin to thank you enough for all you've done. I won't insult you by trying to pay you for your trouble. Or for all those chickens. But I owe you, and I won't be forgetting it. Anything you or anybody in your family needs, anything or anytime, you just call out. I'll damn sure be there."

Keng nodded and extended his hand. "Good luck." After the two men shook hands, Keng said, "Do try to avoid brigands and road agents from now on, would you? They can be hard on a man's health." The farmer laughed and shook his lines to get his buggy horse started. He wheeled around in Wilson's yard and headed back down toward the public road.

Wilson stood watching the buggy drive away. After

a few moments he turned and winced as he slowly, laboriously climbed the rough-hewn steps onto his own tiny porch. All morning he had been trying to hide the effort—and the pain—it cost him to walk. His left hip and leg continued to be painful whenever he put weight onto the leg or had to lift it. Still, nothing was broken. And he learned while he was in prison that pain can be, if not ignored, then certainly endured.

Once he reached the porch he turned back around. Leonard Keng's buggy was barely visible now, the bulk of it hidden by a fold of brown earth. Beyond and below that the land spread in rolling folds with the dark green slash of the Fox River at the bottom and miles upon miles of tan and gray-green grazing lands beyond. This, he thought . . . this was beauty.

Wilson was smiling when he turned back around and thumbed the patented steel latch he had installed on his front door.

He stepped inside and the smile became instantly a frown and then, as quickly, a look of unbridled rage.

CHAPTER FIFTY-THREE

His cabin was not the way he'd left it to go down to
church two Sundays back. It had not been trashed. If
anything it was cleaner now than when he was last
here. But . . . someone had been there. He was sure of it.

The chair that Wilson always haphazardly left
wherever it sat was now pushed tidily beneath the
table.

The coffeepot that he was sure he had left sitting on
the table along with the cup he had used that morning
was now sitting on the stove, and the cup had been
pushed to the middle of the table. He customarily left
it near the edge, on the side of the table he preferred,
the one that faced the door so in fair weather he could
leave the door open and see down toward the river
bottom from the comfort of his own kitchen.

The real proof came when he tried to move some of
the piled-up tins that held his consumables, things
like his flour and salt and sugar, things like coffee and
saleratus and lard. The tins were empty. Or very close
to it.

Someone had been inside this house, came sneaking
in while he was laid up—must have known of his in-
jury to make themselves so bold, perhaps even caused
his injuries—and nearly cleaned him out of food.

Dammit, Wilson grumbled to himself, he would

have given food to a hungry man. Would have been pleased to.

But to steal it? Lyle Wilson could not abide a thief.

He took in a sharp breath at the thought of how that would sound if he said it aloud. He, a convicted thief with a prison record to prove it, could not abide a thief.

Yet it was true. The prison years notwithstanding, Lyle Wilson had never in his life stolen anything.

He had been convicted of stealing half a dozen yearling steers belonging to the Slash S. Bradley Thom and two other Slash S hands had sworn under oath in a court of law that they found the steers in a cirque high above Wilson's property. The steep-walled bowl nurtured a stand of thick, healthy grasses on its sloping bottom and held a small, almost perfectly round pond near the head. The pond was fed by water rushing out of the rock above. It's outflow formed the creek that ran past Wilson's house.

Wilson knew about the cirque but had no reason to go there except once or twice a year, if he felt like hunting a deer or perhaps one of the shaggy mountain sheep that sometimes came down to forage and to drink there. Because of a spill of broken rock scattered on the mountainside below it, he considered the area too difficult for his cattle to reach and never drove them there.

Whoever stole those beeves obviously knew about the bowl too and had hidden the stolen animals there, probably until they could be driven on to sell. In Mexico perhaps or to the army at one of the forts that lingered on in the territory despite the coming of peace, or to one of the several Indian agencies that huddled close by the army posts. There was always a market for beef. Anybody's beef.

He had more than enough time while in prison to think over the details of his trial and he wondered now why neither the prosecutor nor his joke of a defense attorney had bothered to ask just how Thom and those other Slash S riders came to visit that cirque.

During the trial none of them had said anything about following a trail left by the cattle. If they had he would have challenged the statement, because the slope beneath where the cattle was found was too rocky to take tracks.

Wilson still did not know how the riders had come to be there and to find the cattle. What he did know for certain was that Bradley Thom lied when he said he saw Wilson crossing over the Fox with six head of Herefords. The cattle were too far for him to read the Slash S brand on them or he would have raised an alarm at the time, Thom testified, but he was positive it was Lyle Wilson who was driving them.

Thom's testimony, coupled with the fact of the cattle having been found on Wilson's land, was enough to convict him of a crime he did not commit. He had been bitter about that then. He still was.

And now some son of a bitch had stolen nearly all the food he had in the house.

Lyle did not at all mind someone coming in and making himself a meal. He would be glad to feed any hungry man who came to his door. But for someone to come in and just take everything . . .

Oddly enough, his shotgun stood untouched in its corner, as did the boxes of shells resting on a nearby shelf. If anything was going to be stolen he would have thought that would be the first thing taken.

And suddenly remembering, he looked . . . There was still a roll of bills tucked away in an empty coffee can. That was fifty dollars or thereabouts. It was untouched.

He knew what he would spend it on though. He would have to drive down to town and replenish his food supplies.

But not today. Right now he just wanted to go sit on the porch—his very own porch, thank you—and look out across the land while he rested his bones.

Everything else could wait.

Well, pretty much everything else, but not quite. Wilson knelt in front of his stove and pulled the firebox door open, ready to start a new fire. He did not have to. Whoever took all his food had been thoughtful enough to lay the makings for a fresh fire. All he had to do was touch a match to it and the splinters took off with a rush, and soon thereafter the bigger pieces began to catch as well.

Wilson checked the coffeepot that sat atop the stove and found that it too was prepared ready for its next use, with water and ground coffee beans ready to heat. He pushed the pot into the center of the stove top and limped back outside to sit while he waited for the coffee to boil.

He had been robbed. But it was still almighty good to be home.

CHAPTER FIFTY-FOUR

"Good morning, Lyle. How are you feeling now?"

"A little sore, but at least I'm still getting around, Jim." To ease the weight on his aching hip Wilson leaned against a display table piled high with denim trousers.

"You can say you're a little sore if you like but you look like you're still hurting. Surely the drive down here had to hurt."

Wilson shrugged. "Couldn't be helped."

"All right. You know your own mind, Lyle. What was so important that you came down today?"

Lyle Wilson grinned, ignoring a jolt of sudden pain that shot through his left leg. "It's a bad habit I picked up a while back, Jim."

The storekeeper's eyebrows went up.

"Eating," Wilson said.

"I, uh, don't understand, Lyle."

"I got no food in the house, Jim. I had to come down an' get resupplied. Need pretty much everything, same as when I first got home."

"I'm not one to pry, Lyle, but I sold you enough already to last a man a month. Now you say you've used it all?"

"No, sir," Wilson said with an emphatic shake of his head. "I never said I used it. I said it's gone. There's a difference."

"Something happen up there, Lyle?"

"Yes, sir. While I was laid up over at the Moores' place, some son of a bitch came in an' took nearly everything I had in the house."

"I'm sorry to hear that, Lyle."

"At first I thought it was somebody as thought I needed to be taught a lesson, me being a jailbird an' all. But it couldn't hardly be that, because whoever done it was real tidy about it. Those cans you gave me to store stuff in, for instance. They were cleaned out or close to it, but the lids were put back on nice an' tight and the cans were stacked back in the same places where I had them. There was water and coffee beans in the pot on the stove, all set for the fire to start it boiling, and there was a fire laid in the stove ready to touch off. I had a little money left there but it wasn't touched. Now what kind of burglar would take a bunch of food but leave cash money laying there?"

"That's a mystery, Lyle. I got to agree with that. You need most everything again, do you?"

"Yes, sir, I do. I parked my wagon at the dock. If you'd start filling it, Jim, I'll go down to the bank and get the wherewithal to pay you for it.

"Thanks, Jim."

The storekeeper opened his mouth to speak, then thought better of it and began fussing busily at something under his counter.

"What is it, Jim? You were about to say something just then."

"I, uh, I was going to say something about my grandchildren—Harriet has them for the day—but then I thought . . . realized, I mean . . . I didn't mean to cause you any hurt, Lyle. I'm sorry."

Wilson took a deep breath and squared his shoulders. His face, which had been animated and full of interest, became set and hard, without expression. He reached into a pocket and withdrew a scrap of paper. "I've made a list." He limped across the puncheon floor to the counter and handed the list across.

Hanson glanced at the list and said, "This will take a while, Lyle. I'd invite you to come into the kitchen and wait there, but—"

"That's all right, Jim. Thanks, but I'll just go have a bite of lunch after I've been to the bank."

"Fine. That will be just fine. I have some canes here, Lyle. Would you like to borrow one? For the day, or until you're feeling better, if you like."

"No, but thank you." Wilson turned away, stumbled and had to grab hold of the display table to keep himself from taking a tumble. He swung back toward Hanson. "Could I change my mind about that, Jim? Maybe I could use the borrow of a walking stick."

"Of course. I have three of them. Here you go. Take your pick."

Wilson felt quite the dandy when he proceeded on down Main to the Stockman's Bank of Fox Hill.

CHAPTER FIFTY-FIVE

It took little time at the bank to complete Wilson's withdrawal—too little time, actually, leaving him with nothing to do but wait—so he walked on down to the bridge end of Main where Pablo Montez sold his burritos.

The old man greeted him with a gap-toothed grin. "Senor Lyle. Welcome."

"Thank you, Pablo. How are you today?" The two exchanged pleasantries for several minutes while Montez prepared Wilson's order for three of the spicy bean and lamb wraps.

"You are eating your own cabrito, you know," Montez said when he handed the burritos over.

"My . . . Oh." Wilson smiled. "I almost forgot. When did you see Luis?"

Montez shrugged. "A week. Maybe more. Maybe less. He came down. Sold me three wethers. I pay him for them. Is that all right? We talked about this. Always before I pay Luis but that was because the patron, Senor Donovan, lived so far away. Luis would collect the payment and use it to purchase his supplies for the wagon. You live close. And you said to Luis that you would buy his necessary things. Do you want me now to pay you instead of to Luis?"

Wilson slapped his own forehead and grumbled, "Shit, I clean forgot about the stuff I promised Luis. Didn't put his things on my supply list over at the mercantile. Now I need t' go back over there and add that to my order."

"Next month," Montez said.

"What about next month?"

"Next month you buy the things for Luis. This month he has what he takes from your house."

"What the hell?"

"You did not know?"

Wilson shook his head. "I sure did not. I thought I was robbed."

"Robbed? Oh, no, senor. Luis, he knows you are sick. Lying in the padre's house. You can not get out. Can not do the necessary things. And he has no money, no credit at the store. So he went inside your house and took the foods from there."

Wilson barked out a short laugh. "That would explain it. Why things were left so neat even though they were empty. I clean forgot about Luis an' what he needed."

"It is all right, senor? You are not angry?"

"Good Lord, no, Pablo. I am not angry. What I am is relieved. I'm glad the mystery is cleared up and there hasn't been a crime after all."

"Then it is good." Montez waved away Wilson's attempt to pay him for the burritos. "The meat is yours."

Wilson shook his head. "No, you paid for it. It's yours. And I'm not going to start eating free off o' you, old friend. I'll pay you for what I take and I'll thank you for the kindness of your offer." He laughed again. "But I sure wish Luis had left a note or something."

Montez shrugged. "I do not think Luis can write."

"Anyway, I'm relieved to know what happened." He paused, chewed, then grinned. "You sure do make a fine burro, Pablo."

CHAPTER FIFTY-SIX

Wilson came bolt upright on his lumpy, grass-stuffed mattress. He was groggy and disoriented, a deep sleep disrupted by a pounding on the door. He had no idea what time it was. The middle of the night. That was as close as he could guess.

"Open up!" The voice was harsh. Wilson thought he should recognize it but he could not. "Hurry up, dammit."

"Who's there?" Wilson called back.

His nocturnal visitor cursed and pounded on the door some more, then shouted, "Open up or I'll break the sonuvabitch down."

Wilson stood, his head reeling. It felt like gremlins had crept in during the night to stuff cotton wool where his brain should have been. "I'm coming."

"Are you gonna open this door or not?" the voice howled.

In a louder voice Wilson called, "I said I'm coming. Give me a minute." He stood, leaned against the wall until his head stopped spinning. After a moment he chuckled softly. Just think how much worse this would feel if he had been drinking, he told himself.

"Are you going to—?"

"I said I'm coming, dammit." He felt around for the lantern he had placed atop an overturned bucket, found a match lying next to it and lighted the lantern. The noise at his door continued.

Wilson padded barefoot across the floor to the recently hung door and lifted the stout wooden bar from the brackets that held the door closed despite the pounding. He turned back and got his lantern in one hand and a cudgel—it was really a length of split aspen—in the other.

"All right. You can come in now."

The door rattled but did not open.

"Turn the knob, you idiot. It's latched shut."

The knob rotated, the metal tongue withdrew and the door was forceably shoved inward. Wilson held the lantern high with one hand. He held the cudgel down beside his thigh with the other.

"Oh. It's you. What d'you want?" he demanded.

"Checking up on you, jailbird. That's what I'm doing," Marshal Bradley Thom growled. "Step aside."

"What the hell time is this?"

"What do you care what time it is? We're here for a legal and proper search of the premises."

We. Wilson hadn't noticed the two deputies, men he did not know, who stood on his front porch behind Thom. Both of them carried shotguns, and both guns were leveled. There was not enough light for him to see if the guns were cocked but he did not care about that. Not at the moment. The sight of those scatterguns scared hell out of him, without knowing that last little detail.

"Outside," Thom ordered, jerking his head in that direction for emphasis.

Wilson hesitated for only a moment. He had not the slightest doubt that Thom would tell his men to fire with no provocation whatsoever. And if they did the shooting, Marshal Thom would have complete exoneration in the matter. Anything that happened would be the deputies' fault.

Wilson tossed his aspenwood cudgel aside and took the lantern with him when he stepped out onto the porch. He was careful to show that his right hand was empty and that he had no weapons visible.

"Turn around. Assume the position," Thom ordered.

Wilson swallowed back an impulse to resist, set the lantern down and turned to face the cabin. He spread his feet wide and leaned against the two sides of the doorjamb.

"Move away from the door."

Wilson straightened and meekly did as he was instructed. He leaned both hands against the wall, feet wide and well out from the base of the wall.

Thom stood aside while one of the deputies—at least Wilson assumed both men would be duly authorized deputies acting on the sheriff's authority—gently let down the hammers of his shotgun and set it down.

Lordy, Wilson thought. The son of a bitch had been cocked.

The deputy quickly, but none too thoroughly, frisked Wilson. The man did not act like this was something he was accustomed to doing. If he ever went to work in a prison they would teach him better than that. Not that Wilson was complaining. He had nothing to hide anyway.

"Nothing," the man reported.

"All right, then. You two keep him here. He's a tricky bastard, so watch him all the time."

"Yes, sir."

Wilson could see that Bradley liked being called "sir" by the hired help. Liked it awfully well.

"I won't be long. I need to look inside." Without asking for the loan, Thom bent and picked up Wilson's lantern. He carried it inside and closed the door behind him, leaving Wilson and the deputies in the dark. Very dark, after the relative brightness of the lantern.

"Mind if I sit down?" Wilson asked. Then he remembered his prison training and added the obligatory *sir*.

"Yeah. Go ahead."

"Thank you, sir."

Had he been so inclined, Wilson knew, he could have pulled out a concealed pistol—if he had a pistol to conceal—and shot down both deputies. It was their good fortune that he had no such yearnings. He edged sideways until he encountered his rocking chair, turned it to face back toward the doorway and sat. The guards remained standing, shifting from one foot to the other and back again.

Inside his home he could hear Bradley rampaging through his few possessions, probably spoiling half his foodstuffs while he was at it.

That did not matter. Brad was not going to get his goat. Not in such a cheap and juvenile way as this, he wasn't.

But Lyle could continue to think of the Fox Hill town marshal as a shit and a son of a bitch. There was nothing in the law to prohibit that.

CHAPTER FIFTY-SEVEN

By the time Thom and the deputies left, there was a saffron glow of the coming dawn spreading across the horizon to the east. To the west there was a dark cloud bank that held a promise of rain. An empty promise? That remained to be seen.

Wilson picked up his lantern from the porch where Thom had left it and carried it back inside. The clutter was actually not as bad as he had expected to see there. Everything was disarranged but nothing seemed to have been destroyed. The door to the firebox of his stove was open and there were ash and clinkers spilled onto the floor. Apparently Thom had even looked underneath the ashes for whatever he thought he might find.

The man never had said what he was looking for, and if there was a warrant he did not display it. Not that he needed a warrant, not to search the premises of a felon who was free on parole. It would be several years yet before Wilson could feel free to plant the toe of his boot in Bradley Thom's balls. Wilson looked forward to that day. All the more so because in prison he had learned how to fight dirty.

Imagining Marshal Thom's surprise when he discovered the tricks Lyle had learned—and feeling them applied to his person—was something that could keep Wilson amused practically for hours on end.

He put things back in order, swept up the mess on the floor and laid a new fire. Once it was burning he set a pot of water on for coffee and sliced some smoked hog jowl into a skillet. While that was heating he mixed up the batter for some pan bread and put first a dollop of lard and then his batter into the bottom of a pot, since he only owned the one skillet and it was already in use.

The better part of an hour later Wilson carried a filled plate and a steaming cup of coffee out onto the porch so he could eat there where he could look down over his land. And the magnificent view of the Fox and the grassland beyond it. The Bradley Thoms of the world be damned. It was good here. Lyle Wilson wanted nothing better.

But it would be nice to be left the hell alone so he could enjoy it.

CHAPTER FIFTY-EIGHT

"I'll be done here in a few minutes. Could I have a word with you then please, Lyle?"

"Of course, Evan. Anything you like. You know that."

The congregation was filing out of the church at the end of the service, Pastor Moore standing at the door shaking hands and speaking with as many of the churchgoers as he could. Lyle, freshly washed, and his hair slicked down for the occasion, stepped over to the side and waited until the flow of people slowed to a trickle and then stopped altogether. Evan motioned for Lyle to join him and the two stepped back inside the foyer.

"I have a favor to ask of you, Lyle."

"Whatever it is, I'll do it. Just tell me what you want, Evan. You know I owe you for all you've done for me, taking care of me like that. Of course I'll do it."

Moore smiled. "Don't look so worried, Lyle. I don't think it will be too burdensome a chore. The problem is that I've been invited to eat dinner with the Parkers this afternoon and Eva . . . frankly, Lyle, she just doesn't want to sit with me this time. Young Randolph has a crush on Eva and he is really quite a pest about it. He even tries to kiss her."

Lyle tried to stifle a laugh but was not entirely

successful. "Good Lord, Evan, the boy is . . . what? Thirteen?"

"Oh, he's harmless. Eva knows that. But still he bothers her unmercifully. It would be a huge favor to both of us if I could explain to the Parkers that Eva has promised to take her dinner with, well, with you."

"You know I'll do it, Evan, but I should warn you or maybe should warn Eva that all I brought today was a bunch of pan bread and a can of peaches."

"Eva has a basket already packed with everything you two could want."

"I guess that pretty much takes care of everything."

"Yes. Excellent. But, um, there is one more thing."

"Name it," Lyle said.

"You know the way we all congregate in the grove and wander back and forth. Eva is afraid if she is anywhere in sight, Randolph will see her and come to wherever she is. He'll be after her like a fly on honey."

"So what do you have in mind to keep the boy away?" Lyle asked. "Should I punch him? I could do that. Or throw him down and tie him up. That would work. At least until he got himself loose." He apologized, "I'm not too good at tying knots, you see."

Moore laughed. "Eva has that figured out too. She has a lunch for the two of you all packed in a basket. She was thinking, if you wouldn't mind, the two of you could drive down the river for a piece. Find a nice shady spot along the bank and stop there to eat. Would that be all right?"

"That would . . . that would be just fine," Lyle said, his heart beating faster as he said it.

CHAPTER FIFTY-NINE

It could not have been a finer day. Crisp with just a hint of fall in the air. A few cotton-ball clouds floating lazily overhead. Surrounded by mountain, plain and dark water chuckling over the remains of a long-unused beaver dam. And Eva.

Evan's sister—Lyle could not believe, now, that he had been so convinced she was the pastor's wife—was positively radiant. She seemed not to know that. But Lyle did.

She sat close beside him on the seat of his wagon, and he wished he had had the foresight to buy a narrower rig. A buggy perhaps, with a top that could be raised. Or raised halfway so as to form a sort of curtain blocking off the rest of the world. On a narrower seat they would perforce have had to sit close enough to exchange the warmth of flesh barely covered with thin cloth.

Eva's hand lay in the gap that did exist between his thigh and her . . . um . . . limb. Her hand was small. Delicate. And it would have been so tantalizingly easy for him to place his own hand over hers. The bay would follow the road quite naturally with only one hand on the lines. But Lyle was sure she would take offense if he did such a thing. Perhaps she would equate him with the nuisance young Randolph Parker had become. Perhaps to the point of demanding that he turn around and take her home before they even found a suitable picnic site. Lyle did not want to jeopardize the pleasure of Eva's company in exchange for the much greater but less certain pleasure of holding her hand. As things now stood he could look forward to having her companionship for himself, and himself alone, the remainder of the afternoon. He should be satisfied with that.

But he wanted more.

"Up there," Eva said. "In those trees." She pointed toward a stand of cottonwoods a half mile or so ahead. "That looks thick enough to hide us from the road."

"You aren't afraid the Parker boy will . . ."

She laughed. "No, I'm not worried about Randy. His parents will keep him close. I just thought it would be nice to have our picnic where passersby can't see. Do you mind?"

"No. Of course not." Lyle smiled. "We'll take a look when we get closer and see how it looks from the road." He shook the driving lines—with both hands on them—and clucked to the bay. She picked up the pace to an easy trot that made short work of the distance to the thick copse.

"Whoa now, girl." Lyle rolled his fists back and the mare slowed and quickly stopped. He looked over the fringe of the road and turned the bay mare off the roadway toward the trees.

"Wait here a minute please, Eva."

Lyle climbed down from the wagon and walked the slope between the road and the thicket. There was nothing on the ground that would risk either the mare's legs or the wagon's wheels, but the trees and the brush were too dense for him to drive the wagon all the way down to the riverbank. He went back to the wagon and reported what he saw.

"Is that a problem?" Eva asked.

"It is if you want the wagon to be hidden from the road."

"Oh, I don't care about that," she said. "Just so we don't have to have people staring at us when they go past."

"Now, that is not a problem." Eva started to climb down but he stopped her. "Wait there. Let me get us off the road first."

Lyle took the mare's lines in one hand and walked ahead, leading her down to the near fringe of the copse. "This should do."

He got the hobbles from the floor of the wagon and fitted them onto the mare's legs, then left the harness in place but unbuckled her from the poles so she could graze on the dry tufts of grass if she wished.

He walked back to Eva's side of the wagon and reached up for her. She took his hand and stepped over the side of the box. Lyle placed a hand on her waist to help steady her. He could feel the warmth of her through the thin cloth. Could feel her body move beneath his hand. A rush of desire so acute it was almost painful washed through him. He struggled to keep from showing it.

Eva reached the ground and turned to face him. Her body was close. Her lips were even closer. Her eyes seemed huge and moist and sparkling.

"I, uh . . ." He stepped quickly back. "I'll get the basket."

Eva smiled and nodded. "Yes. Thank you." Then she turned and began walking down toward the river, in search of a comfortable spot for their picnic.

CHAPTER SIXTY

Late that evening Lyle added wood to the firebox on his stove and absently closed the door, his thoughts far from his house. He fetched his cup off the table and poured coffee, then paused to drape a blanket over his shoulders before carrying the coffee outside.

The night was clear and cold. The Milky Way was a silver road in the sky, the clarity of the stars somehow brighter on these crisp nights. In the stillness he could hear the mare moving about in the corral and he could see her form, dark against the pale gray of the starlit land. Lyle could see his breath when he exhaled. He was . . . content. Mostly.

He pulled his chair close to the edge of the porch and settled there with his coffee and his thoughts.

His thoughts were focused on Eva Moore and their picnic. Lyle smiled, amused with himself. He could not for the life of him remember what they ate.

He was sure they did eat. Certainly they did. He clearly recalled sitting on the blanket Eva brought, her picnic basket between them. Her face so perfect. Her figure so . . . Lyle tried to avoid remembering that. It was a losing effort. But what they had eaten? He just could not remember.

He remembered the exact play of light and shadow

across the softness of Eva's cheek as a breeze ruffled the leaves overhead.

He remembered the exact curve of her eyelashes.

He remembered the gentle touch of her hand when she passed him a folded napkin containing biscuits, real baking-powder biscuits so light it was a wonder they didn't float out of the cloth as soon as Eva opened it. It had been many years since he'd had biscuits that good.

He remembered the sound of the river.

He remembered the strand of hair that escaped and fell so daintily over her temple. The curve of her lips and the bright, almost startling white of her teeth. The shape of her ankle and lower limb, briefly exposed when she settled onto the blanket opposite him. Remembered the bell-like timbre of her voice. The shape, so soft and vulnerable, of her throat.

Her throat. Oh, Lordy. He remembered the way her dress gapped open a little at the throat when she leaned forward to take something from the basket. Remembered the hollows of tender flesh there. And the swellings.

It had been a memorable day. And Lyle could scarcely remember parts of it, as if he had floated through the day in a fog and only now could try to put it all together in his mind like a picture puzzle made out of brief memories.

But that was all right. It—being with Eva—was the best day he had had since . . . perhaps the finest day he had ever had.

He raised his cup and swallowed. The coffee was already growing cool. That was fine. Lyle did not mind that or much of anything else. He truly was content.

CHAPTER SIXTY-ONE

Lyle stood back. Looking. Examining. Trying to judge weights and angles. And wind. Wind, if there was any, would have an effect too. Finally he grunted, stepped forward and picked up his ax. He needed to make the first cut just . . . there. Exactly there, so the tree would topple precisely . . . there. Good.

He knelt beside and very slightly uphill, then swept the ax sideways so that it bit deep into the trunk of the mature aspen. Aspen was not the best wood for heating. It burned faster, left less in the way of coals and gave off less heat than the other hardwoods. But aspen was what he had the most of. And it replaced itself quickly, the tree growing much faster than most. Besides, it left much less in the way of dangerous tars that could cause chimney fires the way pine will do.

Wilson spent much of the morning dropping aspen trees and chopping the limbs off. Using the ax to cut notches that would determine in which direction the tree fell, then using a saw to slice into the trunk opposite and slightly above the notch to drop the tree, then back to the ax for the smaller limbs and the saw for the big ones. When he was done he would have several dozen clean trunks. He would cut those into lengths his wagon could handle and take them down to his house, where the sawbuck would allow him to cut and split them into stove lengths.

The hard physical labor felt good for a change. Sweat, he sometimes thought, was the oil that a man's body needs in order to operate most efficiently.

Around noon he stopped long enough to eat some cold bacon and corn dodgers, then switched from the felling and limbing to cutting the trunks down to manageable size. Finally he loaded those onto the wagon— more loads would be needed to carry it all down, but that would be for another day—and backed the mare into place between the poles.

Much of the way back would be downhill, so he rigged a chain on the back of the wagon and a hefty log on the other end to act as a brake to keep the wagon from running up onto the hocks of the bay. Wilson took his tools up to the driving box and climbed up into the seat.

"Time to go home, girl," he said as he took up the lines. The mare snorted and tossed her head and then leaned into the heavy load she was asked to pull.

When he got there he found a saddled horse tied to a corral post. He dropped the wagon behind the shed—he could unload it in the morning, as by now it was nearly dark—and led the mare around to the front of the house.

"Hello, Lyle." Leonard Keng was relaxing in the chair on the porch. "You look like a man who's been working."

"What was it made you think that? The sweat or the sawdust? And by the way, hello your own self." Lyle laughed and walked the bay first to the trough, where she drank, and then on into the corral. He stripped the harness off of her, pulled the gate poles over the gap and draped the harness on the corral rails so it could dry overnight. Keng remained on the porch. He seemed in no hurry.

"So what brings you down this way?" Lyle asked when he joined his visitor on the porch.

"Just visiting."

"Now why is it that I think there's more to this visit than a sudden desire for the pleasure of my company?"

"You are a suspicious soul, Lyle Wilson. And by the way, Liza sent a poke of fried chicken for you. I put it inside."

"Thank her for me, please. And suspicion is one of the things I learned in prison. So what is it that brings you here? Not that I mind, understand. I enjoy the company but I have to wonder."

"Can we go inside, Lyle? It's getting chilly now the sun's going down. Let's get the fire going. Put on a pot of coffee."

"All right. You go ahead in. I'm gonna go down to the trough and wash off a bit first. I'll be in in a minute."

Keng nodded and unfolded himself from the chair. Lyle headed down to the water trough to sluice off some of the remnants of his day's labor.

CHAPTER SIXTY-TWO

By the time Wilson came inside, Keng already had a fire going and water on the stove to heat. An oilskin pouch filled with chicken pieces fried Southern style sat in the middle of the table, and Keng had taken two cups down from the shelf and set them out ready for use.

"Looking at the way you have things ready," Wilson joked, "you'd be considered quite a catch on the inside. Make a man a fine wife."

Keng seemed taken aback by the comment. "Do they really . . . ? I mean . . . is there much of that as goes on?"

"Seriously?" Wilson shrugged. "Some. Not an awful lot though. Most of the inmates are stupid but they aren't evil. Surely you saw that in your ranger days."

"I did," Keng agreed. "Sometimes I purely hated having to bring a man in, but of course that's the job, and a man does what he has to. Say, could I ask a favor of you, Lyle?"

"Of course. Anything."

"That coffee won't be ready for a spell and I have a thirst. Could I trouble you for something to drink?"

"The only other thing I have is water. There's some in the bucket there or I could get you cold water out of the standpipe."

"You don't have whiskey or brandy or anything like that?" Keng persisted.

"I'm sorry, but I don't. Don't have a drop in the house. If you really want some we could ride down to town. I'd be happy to buy your drinks there."

"Ha!" Keng barked. "You don't keep any liquor in your house."

"What's so remarkable about that?" Wilson asked.

Keng pulled a pipe out of his pocket and began the process of filling it with tobacco from a pouch he found in another pocket, then tamping the tobacco with his thumb and finally striking a long kitchen match to light it. When he was satisfied that the pipe was drawing well he said, "There's a rumor going around that now you're out of prison you've turned to drink."

"Really?"

"Mm. There's some who say you sit up here brooding and drinking and looking for ways to get even. Mind though, they don't say who you're supposed to get even with. Or exactly why."

"I'm . . . I guess in a way I'm not surprised," Wilson said. "In another, I am. A little anyhow." He sighed. "More hurt than surprised. Hurt that people think of me that way. I should have expected it, I guess. After all, I am an ex-con. That isn't anything I can deny. Everyone around here knows it."

"Yet you came back. You could have gone someplace where no one knew you. You could have started over."

"This is my home," Wilson said. "And anyway, the truth is, I've done nothing wrong, nothing to be ashamed of. If no one else knows that, or cares, I do. And for what it's worth, I don't have any sorrows that I want to drown. Do I have bitterness?" He shrugged. "Sure. Some. But I can put all that behind me. I don't dwell on it all that much."

The former Arizona Ranger puffed on his pipe and nodded. "I've seen a lot of bad men, Lyle. Brought a good many of them in to answer for their crimes and, yes, I've killed some of them when I had to. I think I know a little bit about criminals and about drunks. You don't strike me as being either, which is why I came out here this afternoon. I wanted to see for myself. Come tomorrow I'll be spreading a different sort of word about you, and it won't be any wild rumor, just fact. You can count on that."

"You came all this way just for that?" Wilson asked.

"I suspect you would do as much for me or my boys."

"I got to admit that I'm touched, Leonard."

Keng smiled. "Bubba," he corrected.

"All right. Bubba it is." Wilson stood. "I think the coffee is boiling now. How's about you join me for a cup and for supper too." He laughed. "I have some right-fine fried chicken to offer."

"I accept. If, that is, you're sure the chicken is good."

"I guarantee it." A friend, Lyle was thinking. Damned if he hadn't found a friend here. And a lawman at that, or used to be. How about that.

CHAPTER SIXTY-THREE

"You're awfully quiet this morning," Sarah Thom said, leaning over her husband to pour a second cup of coffee for him. She was not frightened though. Sometimes—often, in fact—Bradley's silence indicated a building fury that sooner or later would erupt into shouted accusations and flying fists. Except, no, that was not right either. Bradley took some perverted sense of pride in the fact that he never "punched" his wife. Not with a closed fist, that is. He insisted he only "slapped" her with an open hand. Slapped just as hard as he was capable of striking her, but he considered the blows mere slaps since he did not use his fists.

This morning, however, he exhibited none of the brooding menace she had come to dread. His silence today seemed more pensive than angry.

"Thinking," he said, confirming her impressions.

"What are you thinking so hard about?" She set the coffeepot back onto the stove and asked, "Would you like more bacon, dear?"

Thom ignored the offer of bacon and said, "I really want to move up. Up to something better than this town job. It's one thing to be the old man's deputy. It'd be better to be sheriff. Lots more money. Bigger town for you and the boys. Yeah, I think we'd all like that. And after that, who knows? Sky's the limit.

"But I need . . . a boost, I s'pose you'd call it. Something to help my image with voters from outside Fox Hill. Town marshal wouldn't be much of a recommendation to most folks. Not unless I captured some famous criminal or something." Thom took a swallow of the hot coffee and said, "I changed my mind about that bacon. Let me have some. A couple of those biscuits an' the bacon drippings too.

"Anyway . . . Where was I . . . ? Anyway, what I'm thinking too is that I need to have me a cattle spread. Something to put me in with the cattlemen and their hired hands, those of 'em that bother to vote. I think being a cowman myself would go a long way toward getting support from them. And they're important to influencing the vote. They don't carry all the votes nor even most of them, but—and I been studying on this considerable, mind you—they carry a lot of weight even with the town voters. So it would help plenty was I to have a cow outfit of my own."

Sarah scraped the rest of the bacon onto Bradley's plate, broke a pair of biscuits beside the bacon and spooned a generous portion of the hot bacon grease over the biscuits.

"More," he said. "Pour the rest of it over."

She did as her husband instructed and mentioned, "That means we would have to move, doesn't it?"

"Not until I get the office," Bradley said, reassuring her.

"But there isn't any land available around here. Not enough to make a whole new cow outfit. There hasn't been for a long time."

Bradley leaned back and chortled aloud. "No, there damn sure isn't." He winked at her. "Yet."

Sarah returned the now-empty spider to the side of

the stove top and said, "Even if someone wanted to sell, dear, we don't have anything close to enough money to buy a place. And I couldn't ask Daddy for any more. I'm sorry, but I just couldn't. Certainly not enough to buy a ranch and cows and . . . and everything."

"I'm not talking about going to your pa again for help, so don't you fret your head about it. I got something in mind. We're gonna do just fine, Sarah. Do just fine. Just you wait an' see." He was grinning when he picked up his fork and attacked the rest of his breakfast.

Chapter Sixty-four

"Do you think ... that is, um ... if you'd be interested ..."

Eva laughed and said, "Yes, Lyle, I would like to go on a picnic with you tomorrow after services." They were standing on the porch at the front of the manse. Lyle had come into town to pick up some things from the store. And to speak with Eva.

He grinned, glad to be taken off the hook like that. He no longer feared outright rejection when he spoke with Eva. Not really. But he had never found it easy to talk with a girl. That was all the more difficult now that he had a prison record. Lyle was at all times uncomfortably aware of that blemish. The fact did not seem to bother Eva but she surely was exposed to all the things people were likely saying about him.

Not that Lyle actually knew what those things were. Rumors and lies and half-truths, he supposed. One of the things he feared—one of the many—was that Eva would be tarred with his brush. If it became known that she was associating with him, it could be difficult for her in Fox Hill.

Which raised another question. Was she associating herself with him?

The truth was that he wanted her to. And yet he did not want to cause her any hurt.

He wanted to be close to her. He did not want that closeness to taint her.

Two sides of a single coin.

"I, uh . . ."

Eva laughed again and lightly touched his wrist. The slight warmth of her fingertips seemed to sear his flesh with heat. "Can we go to our place again, Lyle? I do so love it there. The sounds of the river and"—she paused—"and everything." He could not help noticing that Eva's face flushed a little when she said that. But then he especially liked the "everything" too.

Lyle nodded and Eva said, "I'll pack the lunch. Could you bring something to drink? I don't think we have anything in the house."

"Sure. I'll, uh, I'll do that."

"Good." She touched his hand again. Held that contact for a moment, then stepped decorously back a pace and peered up at him. "I would invite you in, but Evan isn't here and people might talk. Could we . . . ?" She shook her head. "Tomorrow then."

"Tomorrow."

Lyle pinched the brim of his hat and nodded, then backed away. He damn near toppled down the steps once he reached the edge of the porch. He was paying attention to Eva instead of watching where he was walking. He righted himself, gave Eva an embarrassed shrug and turned so he could make his way back out to the street without falling all over himself. He felt enough of a fool without that.

His step was light as he walked back to Jim Hanson's mercantile, where he had left his wagon. He still had plenty of supplies to meet his own needs but calculated that Luis Santiago would be coming down to be resupplied soon and this time Lyle wanted to be ready for him.

"You're all set, Lyle," Hanson told him when Wilson approached the counter. On Saturdays, when most families and hands came in from the outlying properties, Hanson employed the services of two teenage boys to help him fill orders and load wagons. "Your total comes to twelve dollars and . . . oh, just make it twelve dollars even."

"All right, thanks." Lyle dug into his pocket for his purse, opened it and counted out the amount in paper currency. Some merchants still demanded they be paid in nothing but specie but Hanson had always been willing to accept paper as well. "Oh, I almost forgot. I need something to drink. Something bottled. Soda, maybe?"

"Something soft?"

"Yes, sir."

Hanson grinned knowingly and fetched out two quart bottles of dark birch beer.

"Now, Jim, don't you be thinking . . ."

"Thinking what, Lyle?"

"Aw, nothing." Lyle paid for his birch beer and carried the bottles carefully out to his wagon. He wrapped them in his slicker and placed the resulting bundle out of the way beneath the seat. He checked to see that the load was well distributed inside the wagon box and that the tailgate was secure, then walked to the front of the rig and retrieved the hitching weight. He put that under the seat also and climbed into the wagon. He picked up the lines and shook them to get the mare's attention, then started off for home.

Tomorrow, he was thinking. He would see Eva, would have some time alone with her, tomorrow.

CHAPTER SIXTY-FIVE

On Sunday morning Lyle paid extra attention to his appearance. He shaved slowly, careful to avoid slicing flesh along with the whiskers. Poured a pot of hot water into his bucket and washed his face and underarms, dropped his trousers and washed there too. Wet his hair and slicked it back. He was feeling full of himself when he stepped outside into the crisp, early-morning air.

The mare whickered and trotted to the fence when she saw him. She impatiently pawed at the ground while Lyle fetched a half scoop of grain and poured it out for her. While the horse ate he poured another half scoop into the feed bag and stored that under the seat of his wagon along with the hitching weight that always resided there and the carefully wrapped birch beer he had anxiously stored there before the sun came up.

By the time he had done those things the mare was finished with her breakfast. He ducked inside the corral and draped the harness over the horse before leading her out to the wagon and backing her into the poles. Five minutes later he was perched on the wagon seat and rumbling down the path toward the public highway and Fox Hill.

Evan's sermon that morning was titled "When God

Chooses Your Path" and based largely on the story about Jonah, who was swallowed by a large fish and stayed there three days.

At the doorway, as the congregation filed out after the service, Lyle asked Evan, "Surely you don't believe that story. I mean the whale thing and all that."

"But I do. And it was a fish, not a whale. There's a difference, which God would know even better than you or I. But you're missing the whole point, Lyle. Jonah tried to get out of what he was intended to do. God wouldn't let him. That's what you should think about, not whether it was a fish or a whale that held Jonah in its belly."

"Right. I got that. I was just, um, curious."

"You're probably also wondering where Eva is."

"It occurred to me," Lyle admitted. Eva had been there one moment and gone the next. He had not seen her after the service ended.

"She said she forgot something. Which I have trouble believing, since I think a good half of our worldly possessions are in that basket of hers now. Anyway, she asked could you pick her up at the manse and drive from there."

Lyle smiled. "Of course. In that case can I give you a ride home, Evan?"

"Thank you, but I promised to take my dinner with the Andersons this afternoon."

Lyle gave Evan the obligatory handshake and left the church. He walked over to the grove where he had tied the mare, retrieved her from the picket line and led her back to his parked wagon. He secured the bay between the poles, climbed onto the seat and drove out into the road.

Behind him the parking area was nearly full—a

testament to Evan's popularity—while the town streets were empty at this hour on a Sunday when the businesses were closed. At the far end of Main he could see wagons and horses parked outside the Catholic church but there were no people on the streets.

Lyle made the turn toward the manse. He was just short of the picket fence in front of it when he heard a dull clatter of running footsteps and low-pitched grunts of great effort.

He scarcely had time to turn his head in that direction before they were on him.

CHAPTER SIXTY-SIX

He knew them. Damn right he did. Bannerman and Hart. The bastards! They had testified against him at his trial. Lied through their damn teeth then. And Wilson had little doubt that they were the same sons of bitches who had set upon him in the night just a few months ago. Now they were attacking him in broad daylight, but on a deserted street.

Hart reached the wagon first. He threw himself at the seat, grasping Wilson's coattail and giving it a yank.

Probably Hart expected Wilson to pull back in an effort to resist the strength of the larger man.

Instead Wilson twisted to face Hart and flung himself off the wagon seat directly onto a very surprised Tom Hart.

Wilson was too close to use his fists as he landed onto Hart. He used his elbows instead, smashing his right elbow into Hart's face just above the mouth. Blood spurted and began to flow.

"Hey, dammit!" Hart's partner Bannerman shouted.

Wilson went to the ground with Hart and landed on top of the man, driving the breath from his lungs and forcing him to lose his hold on Wilson's clothing. Wilson jumped up in time to confront Willy Bannerman, who was rushing to his partner's rescue.

Except Bannerman was suddenly the one who needed rescue.

Wilson ducked underneath a roundhouse right hand and buried his fist in Bannerman's gut. Bannerman staggered back two steps. Wilson pursued him, following that first punch with a clubbed fist to the throat that came close to crushing Bannerman's windpipe.

Bannerman doubled over, hand clutching his throat. He began to retch and dropped to his knees.

Behind him Wilson heard Hart scramble to his feet. He spun in time to see Hart come upright.

Tom Hart was bigger. Stronger. Probably the superior fighter in almost every way.

But Tom Hart had not been taught the subtle niceties of fistfighting in the same way that Lyle Wilson had during those years in prison.

Hart charged forward, fists high to block any punch the much smaller Wilson might throw.

Except Wilson did not throw another punch. He did not have to. He watched Hart advance, gauged time and speed and distance . . . and kicked Tom Hart in the nuts just as hard as he could.

Hart's face lost all color. He dropped to the ground and tried to curl himself into a ball, hands much too late locked protectively over his testicles.

Wilson turned to see if Bannerman would be continuing without a partner to back him up. Instead he saw Marshal Bradley Thom coming toward them with a revolver in his hand and his expression hard and ugly.

"Hands up, you son of a bitch. You're on your way back to prison."

CHAPTER SIXTY-SEVEN

"Me! But, dammit, I was . . ."

"You'll be a dead son of a bitch if you don't shut up and turn around right now," Thom shouted. "Up against the wagon. Lean over the wheel. Hands behind your back. Do it!"

Wilson clamped his mouth shut and did it. No hesitation. No complaint. His education at the hands of the prison guards had taught lessons that burned deep. They had scarcely been buried before they leaped to the surface again now. He turned around. Leaned over the wheel. Kept his mouth shut as he put his hands behind his back.

He felt a mind-numbing blow between his shoulder blades. The heel of Thom's hand, more than likely. Accompanying that blow high on the spine was a sharper crack of something hard hitting the back of his head. He thought he heard a faint rattle of metal—chain?—along with that. Thom's handcuffs, he guessed, which the marshal was holding in the same hand he had hit Wilson with.

That guess was more or less confirmed by the feel of a wet trickle—blood, almost certainly—running down the back of his neck and into his shirt.

"Hold 'em still now," Thom ordered. He kicked Wilson's feet wide apart and locked the steel bracelets first onto Wilson's left wrist and then, yanking on his arm hard enough to hurt like hell, onto the right. He squeezed down hard on the ratcheting cuffs just to make sure Wilson would be as miserable as Bradley Thom could possibly make him.

Wilson said nothing. He withdrew into himself, standing silently as he had learned—learned the hard way—behind those stone walls.

Thom took hold of the short length of chain connecting the cuffs and yanked. Only after inflicting that pain did he say, "Stand up. Turn around."

Wilson did as he was told. His heart sank when he turned to see Eva Moore on the other side of the low picket fence that surrounded the church manse. She was watching, wide-eyed, as Wilson was arrested.

"You two. He didn't hurt you that bad. Take off outa here. You can stop by my office tomorrow to swear out complaints."

Tom Hart nodded and left, Willy Bannerman trailing behind like some kind of trained bear.

"Now for you," Thom growled. He poked the muzzle of his revolver into Wilson's belly. Wilson knew what Thom wanted. The bastard wanted to let Wilson know that he, Bradley, was in charge now. He could inflict pain if he wanted to. And very likely he wanted Wilson to cringe and cower before his superior strength and position.

Well, the hell with him, Wilson stubbornly thought. The man could punch and poke all he wanted. Lyle Wilson did not intend to give him the satisfaction of seeing how much any of it hurt.

Then he heard the manse gate slap shut, and show it or not, the pain cut deep, knowing that Eva was seeing all of this.

He heard her footsteps approach, light and quick. He tossed his head to get a hank of hair out of his eyes and turned his face toward her.

She was coming. She looked angry. No wonder that should be so, he conceded. Their picnic was to be as good as a date. And now this. Of course she would be angry.

Eva balled her hand into a fist and Lyle steeled himself to take the blow without complaint. She was entitled to that.

Eva stopped close in front of him. Her gaze searched his face, and he did his best to not flinch away from her anger.

But when she swung it was Brad who she socked. Smacked him good and hard actually, right under his left eye. She hit him hard enough to split the flesh over his cheekbone and get a little flow of blood started.

"Ow, dammit. What was that for?" Thom barked.

"I was watching out the window, Bradley. I saw every bit of what happened and if you don't get those stupid handcuffs off Lyle right this instant I'll go to court and testify for him. I'll have a talk with the town councilmen too. Do you hear me, Bradley? You better be paying attention. Now get them off and do it right now, if you please."

Eva planted her hands on her hips and glared up at Thom, who not only was town marshal, he was a head and a half taller than she was. "Go on, Bradley. Do it."

Thom fumbled in his shirt pocket for a moment and eventually produced a handcuff key that he proceeded to employ to release Wilson, first the right cuff and then the left.

The marshal turned, scowling but silent, and stalked away without another word being spoken.

Eva watched him go, her expression looking as if she had a bad taste in her mouth. A mouth that Lyle thought quite lovely. As Thom rounded the corner out of sight she said, "Be careful about him, Lyle. He's up to no good, him and that crony of his, Charles Darlon."

"Darlon?" Lyle said. "What does he have to do with Bradley?"

"I don't know but I walked past the two of them the other day and they stopped talking when I came near. If I were you I wouldn't have anything to do with either one of them."

"All right, thanks." So much for Lyle's promise to stop by and talk with Charlie. Whatever the man was up to, Lyle wanted no part of it, particularly knowing that he was a friend of Bradley Thom.

CHAPTER SIXTY-EIGHT

"Shh." Eva laid a fingertip—her fingertip—against Lyle's lips to shush him. "You don't have a thing to apologize for. I saw what happened. I was watching for you and I saw every bit of it. Do you know those men?"

Wilson nodded. "I know who they are. They're Brad's friends. I wonder if they're the same two that jumped me in the night that time I wound up here in your house to recuperate. They could be, I think. They took me by surprise that time and I never got a look at them."

"Well, you certainly held you own this time, and then some. Against two of them."

"In prison you . . . learn things."

"Oh, I don't mean to bring all that back."

"No, it's all right, Eva." He shrugged. "It happened. I lived through it and now it's behind me."

"Yes, and I think . . . Oh, Lyle! You're bleeding. Turn around."

He did. He felt the light touch of Eva's hand. Felt her wipe the back of his neck and the top of his right shoulder.

"You have to come inside," she said. He could feel her doing something on the back of his head. Rooting into his hair. "I want to clean this up. Come along now, please."

"But our picnic . . ."

"Can wait," she finished for him. Eva took him by the elbow and tugged. "Come inside. Please."

Lyle had little choice but to follow. The truth was, he would follow Eva Moore anywhere that she wanted him to go.

She took him into the now-very-familiar house and back to the kitchen, where she sat him onto a ladder-back chair and said, "Take off your shirt. I need to clean that."

"Oh, I'm not hurt bad."

"Perhaps not, but I'd like to see that for myself if you don't mind." Eva's voice was crisp and businesslike. "Now please. Off with the shirt."

"I, uh . . ."

"Lyle Wilson! I declare. You're being modest." She laughed. "When you were hurt that time, I bathed you. I don't think it will shock me now to see your naked shoulder."

He flushed bright red when he remembered . . . He quickly unbuttoned his shirt and pulled it off.

"Let me take that," Eva said, solving his problem of what to do with the shirt now that he had it off. "When I'm done with you I'll wash the blood out. If I don't do it soon it will set and leave a stain. Better yet, I'll do it now. You aren't bleeding anymore and this shirt needs tending too."

Lord, she was cute, Lyle thought as he looked up into her face.

Eva poured some water into a basin and immersed his collar and the upper part of the shirt into it, scrubbing the cloth back and forth against itself for a few moments. She poured that water out and replaced it, then scrubbed the shirt collar again.

"There. It's gone." She wrung the shirt as dry as she could and hung it over the other kitchen chair. "This won't take long to dry. Now let me see to you." She found a piece of sponge, dampened it and began oh so gently swabbing the back of his head and, more briskly, on his shoulder and upper back.

"It looks worse than it is," she said. "There's only a little cut on your head. A lot of blood though. Do you think those men will try again to hurt you?"

The sudden change of subject took him by surprise. "I don't know. They might, I suppose. But I don't know why they'd want to to begin with. 'Course, I still don't know why they testified against me at my trial. They lied then but I couldn't see they had any reason to. Now this."

"You must have done something to them," Eva said.

"If I did I don't know about it. Sure don't know how I could've given offense to them. Them and me have never run in the same circles."

"What if they use guns the next time, Lyle? Shouldn't you wear a pistol? Almost everyone does. If they wanted to shoot you, you wouldn't have any way to defend yourself."

"I'm not allowed to wear a pistol." He explained the restrictions of his parole. "The only gun I have now is a shotgun, and I can't carry that on my hip, now can I?"

"No, but you could carry it in your wagon, couldn't you?"

"Sure, I suppose so, but . . ."

"Put your shirt back on, Lyle. We're going to drive out to your ranch and get that shotgun. You're going to carry it with you wherever you go from now on."

Lyle looked at Eva with a mixture of surprise,

amusement and adoration. The preacher's little sister was more feisty than he ever would have thought. And Lord, she was pretty.

"All the way out there? What about our picnic?"

"We'll have it. It's just that now we will picnic at your place. Come on now. We need that shotgun and you need a dry shirt." She took him by the hand and pulled, practically dragging him with her out the door and into the street, where the bay mare was still standing.

CHAPTER SIXTY-NINE

"Bachelors' quarters and boars' nests," Eva exclaimed. "I can certainly see why people speak of them as if they were the same thing."

Lyle colored with embarrassment. Again. "I, uh, didn't know I was gonna have company."

"Obviously," she said. "Sit down now. Right there at the table. I want to have another look at that cut on your head. Then I'll bring in the picnic basket."

"You must be famished," Lyle said. It was late afternoon and he had begun to think his mouth hated his stomach and had gone on strike.

"I want to see to you first. Now change that shirt . . . I won't look . . . and sit down. First your head, then your belly. All right?"

"Whatever you say."

Eva laughed. "You don't have to look so sad when you say that."

"Did you know that you have dimples when you laugh?"

"Do I?" she asked coquettishly.

"And you're awfully pretty." He blushed again now that the thought had become speech.

"Don't be silly. I'm as plain as a mouse and I know it. Evan's little church mouse. That's what they called me back home."

"Then they were out of their minds," Lyle insisted.

"It's sweet of you to say so. Now go change that shirt, then sit down. I'll be right back." She swept out the door before he could move to help her.

He thought about rushing out to see if she needed him for whatever she was doing, then realized that this was probably Eva's way of giving him some privacy. He rushed to remove the damp shirt he had worn to church that morning and replace it with something clean and dry. If he could only find . . . He scattered clean but not-yet-folded laundry until he found a shirt he thought might be suitable, and pulled it on. He had only just begun fastening the buttons when Eva returned lugging the huge picnic basket.

"Wait! You shouldn't be—"

"Hush. I know what I'm doing and I am perfectly capable of doing it. Now sit."

"Yes, but . . ."

With a most unladylike grunt of effort Eva lifted the basket onto Lyle's kitchen table. She turned to face him with a look of satisfaction. A wisp of hair had fallen over her left eye. Lyle thought it adorable but Eva must have found it annoying. She tried blowing it out of the way and when that did not work brushed it back over her ear.

Eva marched across the room until she faced him practically nose to nose. "Well?" she demanded.

"Well, um, well what?"

"Here we are. Not another human being within miles. And you half dressed. No! You don't have to jump like that, and quit fooling with those buttons." She peered up at him. Eva stood so close that he could feel her breath on his neck. His chin. His . . . lips.

She kissed him.

Her lips were soft. Mobile. Very actively involved in the business of kissing. Lyle felt his knees go weak and his head swam.

He wrapped his arms around the girl and kissed her back.

Suddenly he was not as hungry as he had thought.

CHAPTER SEVENTY

Lyle felt strange driving back into town with Eva on the wagon seat beside him. He was sure that anyone who saw them would immediately know that he had spent the afternoon spooning with Miss Eva Moore. He was not sure just how they would know this. But he was positive that they would.

He snuck a glance in her direction and felt his heart swell and his throat tighten. Lordy, she was beautiful. And he was so plain. How could a girl like that want anything to do with a jailbird like him? But oh, he would not give her up, not for anything.

"Lyle."

"Yes?"

She giggled. "You missed the turn. That was my street back there."

He felt his face flush with heat. Lyle pulled the left lead to turn the mare's head and swung her around in a tight turn back the other way. A few minutes later they drew to a stop in front of the manse. There were lights showing at the front windows and no sooner were they stopped than Evan came bolting out of the front door and down the walk.

"Where the devil have you people been all afternoon?" Evan demanded. "I've been worried sick. I thought about calling out the marshal to form a search party."

"Evan, you're being silly," his sister said. "I was with Lyle. I was perfectly safe."

"But where . . . ?"

"We were talking. Now help me down, brother dear. I need to go inside and get our supper started."

Evan frowned but he did not object. He reached up to help Eva out of the wagon and onto the ground. "Good night, Lyle. I had a lovely time today. Thank you." She bobbed her head and turned away.

Lyle ached to take her into his arms one more time so he could give her a proper good-bye, but that was simply not possible. Not here in town with her brother standing right there and who knew how many eyes peering out at them from behind windows and doorways.

Eva let herself in through the gate and went skipping up the walk to the porch. The screen door creaked open and slapped back against the door frame and Eva was gone.

"Lyle? Lyle!"

He shook himself and returned to the present. For a few moments he had been far away in fond reverie. With Eva at his side. "I—I'm sorry, Evan. What were you saying?"

"I was saying that Marshal Thom was looking for you. He said something about there being an altercation after services today?"

Lyle shrugged. "It wasn't anything important. Nothing he needs to be bothered with."

"Do you think you should go talk to him about it?"

"Oh, I wouldn't think so, Evan. It wasn't anything important. I'll see the marshal the next time I'm in town. There certainly isn't any reason to disturb him at his home on a Sunday evening."

"If you say so. Will you come in and join us for supper?"

Lyle shook his head. "Thanks, but it will already be late by the time I get home. Another time perhaps."

"Right. Another time." Moore stepped back from the wagon wheel he had been leaning on while talking with Lyle. He smiled and waved, and Lyle shook the lines to put the mare into a slow walk.

As he drove out of town Lyle was acutely aware of the shotgun that lay on the wagon floor beside his feet.

CHAPTER SEVENTY-ONE

Lyle liked to be on the porch with that first cup of morning coffee when the sun first colored the sky. He rose at his usual hour, stirred up some coals from the overnight fire and added fuel until he had a good blaze purring away in the stove, then set the kettle in place.

It did not take long to get the water warm. He poured some into a basin to use for his shave, dribbled a handful of crushed coffee beans into the kettle and set it back in place on the stove. He turned up the lamp wick to get as much light as possible, whipped his bar of soap into lather and quickly shaved before the water in the basin got too cold for comfort. By the time he finished shaving, his coffee was ready. Lyle draped a blanket over his shoulders, picked up the cup of dark, steaming brew and stepped outside, intending to settle into his rocking chair and watch the sun rise.

Instead he barely got out the door before he stopped short. A ghostly white shape sat between him and the corral. Lyle smiled.

"Luis," he called. "Coffee's hot an' ready if you want some."

A few moments later a spill of yellow light appeared at the back end of Luis's caravan. The Mexican climbed down and approached the porch. "Good morning, senor."

"Come inside, Luis. Let's get you some coffee, then we can sit out here an' enjoy the morning while you bring me up to date."

Thirty minutes and second cups later Lyle was satisfied that his goats were being well tended. Already there had been enough increase by way of late-dropped kids to show a profit, on the books if not in cash.

"And I have heard, Senor Lyle, that the army will buy meat for the *indios*. They wish to buy cows, sheep . . . and the cabrito too. They do this at Overton. A buyer will be there for one month, to begin next month."

"Do we have extra goats to sell, Luis?"

"*Si*, senor. We have the old females too old to give birth. We have the wethers. The young does we will keep, of course, but we have"—Santiago shrugged—"more than a hundred we can sell. Maybe a hundred and twenty, hundred and twenty-five. I will have to look at the old ones again to decide which can stay another year." He took a sip of coffee and smiled. "The army pays as much as three dollars for each goat, or so I have been informed."

Something occurred to Lyle and he asked, "Luis, how the devil do you learn things like that when you're out in the mountains with no people around? I didn't hear anything about it and I'm in town two, three times a week. Where do you get your news?"

Santiago chuckled, his mustache ends bobbing up and down. "The people of the hills, they tell me. We exchange news. Sheepherders, woodcutters, charcoal burners. We see much; we say little. That is good, yes?"

"Could be," Lyle agreed.

"There is one thing, senor. It would be good business to sell to the government, but they would not buy from a poor goatherd like me. They want to do business with the true owner. They would want you to be there to sign the bills of sale. Would this be possible, senor?"

"The buyers are at Overton, you say?"

"They will be, *si*."

"I know how far that is by horseback, but how long is it to take a flock of goats there?"

"I could have the flock there in three weeks of time," Luis said. "You could meet me there if you wish. There is no need for you to go with the goats."

"Three weeks, you say."

"*Si*, senor."

Lyle nodded. "I'll be there, Luis." He stood. "Here. Give me your cup an' I'll get refills for the both of us. We'll enjoy this beautiful morning for a spell; then we can load your supplies. I have them inside."

CHAPTER SEVENTY-TWO

Lyle left the wagon sitting in the yard and saddled the bay instead. Instead of following the wagon road down to the highway, he took the mare up and over the ridge that lay between his place and Fox Hill and made a more or less straight line down to town.

The door of the church was open. Eva might well be in there, cleaning up from the most recent functions, but Lyle rode resolutely past. Business first; the pleasure of Eva's company later.

He took Main down to the other end of town and reined to a halt outside the livery. He stepped out of the saddle and loosed his cinch, then led the bay mare inside.

"Sam? Where you at, Sam?"

"Up here," a voice called from the loft overhead. "Who is it?"

"It's me, Sam. Wilson." He tied the mare to one of the rings on the wall and scratched her poll.

"I'll be right down, Lyle."

"Take your time. I'll wait." He could hear some bumping and banging in the loft above, then Sam's boots and lower legs appeared at the top of the ladder. The rest of the man quickly followed as Sam climbed down to ground level. He offered his hand and a smile. "How can I help you, Lyle?"

"I'm needing another horse, Sam. Something that can pull and pack and ride too."

"Got to be sound, I suppose."

"Yeah, of course. I wouldn't want to buy a critter that's already hobbled."

Arnold scratched his chin and pondered. "I don't have any horses of that sort, Lyle. Not that are broke real good anyway. But could you use a mule?"

"I'd consider one, sure."

"This fella is broke to ride as well as the usual pack or harness. He's stout enough. Mind you, I've never actually saddled and rode him, but I was told he'll ride too. He's no beauty, Lyle, but I'll swear that he's sound. Take him back, no questions asked, if you find anything wrong with him." Arnold laughed. "Other than appearance, that is. I'm not telling you he's pretty."

"How old is he, Sam?"

"I'd say fourteen, for sure no older than sixteen. He should have some good years in him yet."

"I'd look at him, Sam." Half an hour later, Lyle was the owner of a dark gray creature with yard-long ears—or so Lyle swore they were—and practically no tail. He had a muzzle that was pale with age and dark scars on his rump and scrawny hindquarters. The mule stood only fourteen hands high but he was stout and strong. Just as important, Lyle liked the patience and intelligence that he thought he saw in the mule's eyes.

"The halter goes with him?"

"If you want it, it does," Sam Arnold said.

"I do. And would you have a packsaddle as well?"

"That would cost you extra."

"That seems fair."

"You want one?"

Lyle nodded.

"I'll throw in a blanket, but you'll need a crupper and breechin' strap."

"All right."

"Just a minute. I'll go in and figure it all up."

"While you're doing that I'll go to the bank and get some money out so I can pay you."

Arnold nodded and headed for his office. Lyle left the mare tied where she was and walked up the street to the bank. By the time he returned to the livery Sam had the bill of sale written out, ready to be signed.

The two men shook hands again and Lyle mounted the bay and led his mule out onto the street. He still had some shopping to do, so he headed for Jim Hanson's store.

CHAPTER SEVENTY-THREE

Wilson snatched his hat off and stepped out of the aisle. He bobbed his head and smiled. "Sarah. How do." Funny thing, he realized. It did not hurt so much this time. In fact . . . seeing her did not hurt at all now. He looked down at the little boy who clung so tight to her skirt and at the round-cheeked baby in the perambulator. No, it no longer hurt at all.

"How are you, Lyle?"

"Fine, thanks." It was the truth. Another realization. He was content now. "And you?"

She gave him a wan smile and a tilt of her head. He was not sure what he was supposed to take that to mean. "You go ahead, Lyle. I'm just here to see Mama and Daddy. I come by pretty much every day. I mean . . . being so close and everything."

"Yes, of course." Sarah was not as pretty as he remembered.

She noticed him appraising her and obviously mistook his thoughts, for she quickly put a hand over the side of her face and said, "This . . . I fell. It was silly of me."

Lyle had not really noticed the faded bruising this time until she called attention to it. A fall, she said. All right then. A fall. It happens. "You look fine," he lied.

"Would you, um, excuse us please, Lyle? The boys are hungry and I'd rather not open my dress in public."

"Of course." The littler one was dozing and did not at all look like he was searching for the breast, but that was as good an excuse as any. If it was calculated to titillate Lyle or to entice him, it failed. "Good day, Sarah."

"Good day, Lyle."

He let the three of them proceed up the aisle in her father's store and around the counter to disappear into the back rooms. Lyle loitered in the store until Sarah and the children were gone, then wandered up to the counter where her father stood.

"Hello, Lyle. How are you today?"

The two of them went through the usual pleasantries that had to precede any talk of business. Then Hanson asked, "What can I do for you today?"

"I'm wanting a couple of those heavy canvas panniers, Jim. I need to pack some stuff and I am no hand at the art of it. Wouldn't dream of trying to build a soft pack with diamond hitches and the like, so I bought me a pack frame. Now I need the panniers to go with it an' I should be good as gold."

"I have some. One set, you said?"

Lyle nodded. "Yes, sir, and I think I'll treat myself to one of those waterproof bedroll covers and a couple soft quilts to go in it." He smiled. "I never had such luxuries before but I think it's about time that I did."

"I agree with you completely, Lyle. Wait here. I have to go in the back for those panniers. The bedroll covers and the sugans are over there. Pick out what you like. I'll be right back with your panniers."

All he needed now, Lyle thought, was a stop at the

church manse to see Eva for a minute. Or two. Then he would be ready to travel down to Overton to meet Luis and the goats so he could start making some cash profit on his livestock investment.

CHAPTER SEVENTY-FOUR

On his way outside, loaded down with panniers and his brand-new bedroll, Lyle almost bumped into Bradley Thom, who was coming into the store. "Excuse me. I didn't see you," he said.

"Watch yourself," Thom snarled. "Going somewhere, are you? And what were you doing in there? You were looking for a way to see my wife on the sly, weren't you?"

"I was just buying these things. That's all I was doing," Lyle said, eyes down as he had learned to do in prison on the rare occasion when he might speak with a guard.

"That better be all. And don't think I won't find out."

"Yes, sir."

"Get on now. Get away from me."

Lyle turned and hurried off the sidewalk to his horse and mule tied to a rail in front of Hanson's. He set the bedroll down on the edge of the sidewalk boards. The dark twill bedroll cover was clean and bright and new and he wanted to keep it that way, a feeling that was entirely illogical, as the whole purpose of the cover was to be placed on the ground. Lyle knew that. He put it up out of the dirt of the street anyway.

The canvas panniers he draped over the crossed horns on the pack saddle. He tugged and pulled until they hung to his satisfaction and then buckled them in place. The panniers were so much easier to manage than the complicated rope hitch required of professional freight packers, but they did get the job done. Lyle was pleased with them.

Once everything else was secure he settled the light but bulky bedroll on top, between the panniers.

When he moved to the rail to retrieve the lead rope, the mule stretched out its nose and sniffed Lyle's shirt, so he paused to give it a rub underneath its jaw. The animal snorted, blowing a little snot onto Lyle, and tossed its head. Getting acquainted, Lyle figured. He scratched it a little more and rubbed its poll, then took the lead rope in hand and swung onto the mare's back. The mule followed willingly enough when he led the way on the now-familiar route to the manse.

There was no rail or hitching post in the street outside the Moores' home, so Lyle tied his animals to the fence and silently hoped they would not booger and tear a section out. He knew he could trust the mare to stand quiet but the mule was another matter. It he had to take on faith.

Lyle let himself through the gate and stepped up onto the porch. He took his hat off and held it in hand while he rapped on the door.

And waited.

Apparently no one was home.

Lyle mumbled a few cuss words under his breath and went back to the street. He gathered up his mule and mounted the mare.

When he passed the church that door too was closed and no animals or buggies were in the churchyard.

Not that it really mattered, he supposed. Eva knew he would be away for the next week or so. He had told her that almost as soon as he knew himself. But he really would have liked to see her again before he left.

He thought about going back to the house to leave a note. Except it was blocks behind him and out of his way, and anyway he had nothing with him to write on. That would require a return to Hanson's, and Bradley and Sarah might still be there. Lyle would rather not run into them again. Twice in one day would be more than enough.

That last kiss from Eva would just have to be put off until he got back.

He smiled, thinking he would just have to double the kisses he got from her then.

Not that he needed an excuse.

Lyle laughed aloud, feeling good about the future. Anticipation. That, he realized, was something he had not experienced for a very long time. Feeling it now was fine, just fine.

"Come along now, children," he said to his animals. "We've got things to do."

CHAPTER SEVENTY-FIVE

"It was always him, wasn't it?" Thom accused. "It was always that son of a bitch Wilson that you wanted. You scarlet woman. You shameless whore!"

"Please," Sarah pleaded. "Keep your voice down, Bradley. The boys. Think of our boys. Your boys, Bradley. They shouldn't . . . shouldn't hear . . ."

"You bitch," he roared. "Were you plotting against me? Were you? Is that why you were meeting him today? Are you planning to take my boys away with you too? I suppose next you'll be wanting to change little Braddie's name so you can put all memory of me out of your life. Is that it, Sarah? Is it?"

"You're overwrought, Bradley. Let me get you something. A cup of coffee. Would you like a cup of coffee, dear?"

" 'Dear'? Don't you dare call me Dear. You meet with your—what do you call him anyway? Your boyfriend? Your lover? Well, I am your husband, and don't you forget it."

"I would never . . . Bradley, you are imagining things. I wasn't meeting with Lyle, as you put it. I go to Poppa's store almost every day. You know that. It's good for the boys to see their grandparents. Sometimes . . . sometimes I like to talk to my mother. Lord knows, she is just about the only woman in this whole town who wants to talk to me. I go there, yes. Lyle goes there sometimes. The whole town goes there to shop. That doesn't mean I'm there meeting with anyone. It just means they like Poppa. Why are you so touchy anyway? I married you, Bradley. I carried your sons. You are my husband. I've never given you cause for concern. Whatever your fantasies and demons, Bradley, I have been a faithful wife to you and a careful mother with your . . . with our sons. Even if I wanted Lyle back again, he isn't interested any longer. He has someone else now."

"He does? Who?"

"Lyle has been seeing the preacher's sister."

"That little slut Eva?"

"I'm sure Miss Moore is a good girl, Bradley. Even the gossip doesn't imply otherwise."

"A man has to get it someplace, Sarah. If Wilson isn't getting it from the Moore twist, maybe he's getting it from you. Is that it, Sarah? Are you Wilson's whore?"

Sarah reached up and slapped Thom, hard, her hand slashing across his face with enough force to split the side of his lip and start some blood trickling down into his beard.

"Oh, God!" she moaned as the enormity of what she had done reached her. "I didn't mean . . . I didn't . . . Bradley, please, no . . ."

Thom bunched his big hands into fists. His expression turned stony and his eyes held a cold, distant fury.

He was careful to avoid striking her face. His punches—not slaps this time but solid punches—concentrated on her breasts and belly and on her back, and when she fell to the floor he gave off punching her and kicked her instead. He kept it up until he became tired, then went into the kitchen to fetch his own cup of coffee.

CHAPTER SEVENTY-SIX

Two and a half days on the road and two nights sleeping on the hard, cold ground left Wilson bleary-eyed and weary. It was a distinct pleasure for him to stop on the crest of a low hill north of the vast, grassy basin where Overton lay and look down on the bustling activity below.

The town normally was little larger than Fox Hill. Now it was surrounded on all sides by large herds and small, by cattle and sheep and goats. Maybe by pigs too, for all he knew, Wilson thought, rising in the saddle in a vain attempt to take it all in.

The size of the town had been expanded on two sides by tents, one side laid out with military precision and the other haphazard and rowdy. Stockmen had come from far and wide to sell to the army. At least as many soldiers had come to buy and to oversee. Untold numbers of Indians had come to receive their allotments of living meat. And with them all were the gamblers, whores and scoundrels who followed any large gathering of strangers like wolves ready to feast on the unwary.

Excitement and eager anticipation filled the very air, Wilson thought, and he himself was not immune, even knowing the dangers as he did.

He patted his coat pocket to reassure himself that

his poke was intact before he heeled the mare forward, the mule following obediently behind.

Once he reached the outskirts of the town he was swallowed up by it, surrounded by voices—talking, shouting, singing, demanding—and by barking dogs, lowing steers, bleating sheep and—yes, by damn, right over there—pens of grunting hogs as well.

Wilson ignored the offers posed by whores and gamblers and made his way into the permanent section of town, where there were buildings instead of tents. He had to weave his way through traffic. The street was filled with horses and vehicles of every description, red men and white, soiled doves and Negro soldiers in blue uniforms. Dust rose under countless hooves and boot soles. It covered everything and everyone, and no one seemed to mind it in the least. There was too much else to see, to experience, to do.

"Say, mister," Wilson said, leaning down on his saddle. "Where's a good hotel?"

"Good? You won't find good here, friend. Nor cheap. There's only one actual hotel in town an' they charge three dollars a night an' for that you have to share the bed. But you got a soft mattress to sleep on an' maybe not so much noise t' put up with." The man grinned. "That's if you close the window an' settle for the smell of your bed partner. Believe me, that won't be perfume."

"That sounds like the voice of experience," Wilson said with a smile.

"So it is. But I'm havin' fun, I can tell you that."

"Seen any goats hereabouts?" he asked.

"Sure. Seen several herds of them. They're over yonderway," he added, pointing.

"Thank you, neighbor." Wilson touched the brim of

his hat and moved off at a slow walk, slow so he could try to take it all in. There was just too much. Faro tables and shell games, barkers hawking tickets to curiosities and wonders of nature, vendors selling hats and spurs and suits of clothing. It was all too grand and Wilson rode with a smile on his face and a nod toward any who caught his eye.

He passed through town and veered off to his right and indeed found goats. Thousands of them. And the dogs that inevitably accompanied them. He also found a caravan that he thought he recognized.

"Luis? Is that you in there, Luis?"

A head emerged from the back of the caravan. A Mexican, but younger and broader than Luis Santiago. The man stared at Wilson, turned and spoke to someone behind him and then disappeared back inside the caravan. A moment later Luis poked his head out the back door. He looked, then broke into a broad smile of welcome when he saw Wilson. " 'Ey, senor. Come, come now. Let me take those animals. Come join us. We are about to have some lunch, eh? Come share, senor."

Wilson stepped down off the mare and staggered for a moment before he got his legs under him again. He was simply not accustomed to so much riding. His thighs ached, his butt hurt and his legs felt weak and wobbly beneath him.

But the worst of it was over with.

Wilson stuck his hand out to shake with Santiago. "It's good to see you, Luis. Mighty good."

CHAPTER SEVENTY-SEVEN

Luis's young visitor was a goatherd for a gent named Baker from somewhere to the south. Wilson was not entirely clear about all of that, since the youngster, whose name was Elio, spoke practically no English and the few words he had were heavily accented.

It seemed that Luis and Elio took turns watching each other's goats when one of them had to be away from the herds. Exactly why one might want to temporarily leave the company of the goats was something Wilson thought best left unexplored. But looking back toward town with all its diversions, he could think of several reasons.

Lunch was rice seasoned with onion and saffron and peppers. Apparently protocol called for meals to be shared but eating utensils to be one's own. Luis and Elio carried spoons in their pockets. Wilson made do with the large blade of his penknife. The rice, fortunately, tasted much better than it looked.

"Tell me what we need to do here, Luis. Have you already made arrangements to sell our animals?"

"No, senor. That you must do. The goats . . ." He turned to Elio and had a conversation in Spanish, then returned his attention to Wilson. "There is an officer. He sits behind a desk inside the school building. You must go to him."

"Ah, and he buys the goats, is that it?"

Luis shook his head. "No, senor. You are to speak with this man. He will give you an a . . . ap . . . He will say a time when someone will come to inspect the goats."

"An appointment," Wilson said.

"*Si*, senor. That is the word. App . . . what you said. A man will come with soldiers. He will look at the goats. If he sees the animal is healthy and has good flesh, he will say to the soldier with him that it is accepted. That soldier will mark the goat with a color of paint from a can that he carries. Another soldier will write in a book. It is from this book that you will be paid, senor. After the goat is marked, still more soldiers will take it from the herd and take it apart. They will make a new, big herd. From this the *indios* will be given their allotment."

"And after that?" Wilson asked.

"What do you mean, senor?"

"Do they pay in cash? Some kind of check or voucher? What happens after they take the goats away?"

"This I do not know. More food, senor?"

"Thank you." Wilson held his plate out and Luis piled some more rice onto it. Luis spoke to Elio again, the Spanish words flying rapidly back and forth between them.

"Senor, after we eat Elio will watch over all the goats, Senor Baker's and yours too, while I walk into town with you. I will show you the place where you must speak with the officer."

"All right, fine. We'll get this business done quick as we can." He took another huge bite of the rice—or anyway as large as he could get onto the blade of his pocket knife—and smiled. "Good stuff, Luis. Thanks."

Chapter Seventy-eight

There were five men ahead of Wilson in the line to see the purchasing officer, so he had plenty of opportunity to look the room over.

School desks had been shoved over to the side of the room—but carefully lined up—to make a broad aisle, at the head of which was a massive desk that Wilson assumed was normally used by the teacher. On the wall behind the desk was a large American flag hanging over the chalkboard so that all thirteen stripes and forty-six stars were displayed.

The officer seated at the desk had gray hair neatly trimmed and a large, nearly black mustache. He wore his uniform buttoned tight to the collar and sat ramrod straight. He had gold-colored shoulder boards to indicate his rank, but Wilson had no idea what the unfamiliar designs on them meant. A dark blue kepi rested on the desk by his left hand and an open ledger lay under his right. A pen and inkwell were beside the bright green blotter.

Two Negro soldiers, natty in perfectly turned-out uniforms and each as dark as the potbelly stove in the room, stood at rigid attention flanking the desk on either side. These two held Springfield rifles with bayonets attached, snug against their right legs with butts grounded on the schoolroom floor. The guards—if that is what they were—wore their short-billed kepis pulled low over their eyes and with chin straps tight beneath each man's lower lip. It looked uncomfortable.

Another guard, this one a white man with sergeant's stripes on his arms, sat in one of the school desks near the doorway. It was he who controlled the access to the officer.

The line moved slowly. Each rancher engaged in lengthy conversation with the officer, that gentleman posing a series of questions. His expression suggested the questions were rote, that he had little interest in the answers. Each seller produced whatever papers he might have on his animals.

Wilson was not close enough to overhear what was being said by seller or potential buyer, either one. At the conclusion of each conversation, however, the officer wrote something in his book and nodded to the seller to indicate that the interview was complete. The seller then exited the schoolhouse and the sergeant—Wilson at least recognized that the sergeant's three stripes up and three stripes down indicated someone of importance—allowed the next man to approach the purchasing officer.

Wilson wished he had kept Luis with him so that at least he would have someone to talk with while he waited. The men in front of him were grim faced and serious. They did not look like they wanted company.

So he shifted from one foot to another and stared at the floor and waited his turn. Waiting without complaint was another thing he had learned in prison.

Finally it was his turn. "The captain will see you now, sir."

Wilson nodded to the sergeant and walked forward to stand in front of the desk. Without thinking about it he came to the rigid posture he had been taught to use when approaching the warden.

"Lyle Wilson here, sir, down from Fox Hill with a hundred thirty goats to sell."

CHAPTER SEVENTY~NINE

Lyle stopped outside the busy schoolhouse and adjusted the set of his hat, then absently looked around all the bustling activity while he considered. Thursday—it was Thursday, Captain Reynolds said, when someone would come to appraise his stock and, if they were healthy, issue a voucher. After that, Lyle could take his voucher to the paymaster, who was using the services of the First Bank of Overton. That gentleman would give Lyle his choice of receiving cash on the spot or taking his payment in the form of a warrant drawn on the United States Treasury, which Lyle could then take to Cornell Fredericks at the Stockman's Bank back home.

The government warrant, he decided. That would be safer than carrying cash, and once he got to the bank it would be every bit as good as specie. More convenient too.

Lyle lifted his hat to allow a little fresh air under it, then once again adjusted the set of it. He was feeling good and felt like buying a beer for Luis, but he had not come inside the schoolhouse with him and now had disappeared. That probably would have been a bad idea anyway. Mexicans might not be welcome in the Overton saloons, likely were not, and if there was anything Lyle did not need it was trouble.

Bradley Thom would like nothing better than an

excuse to find Lyle in violation of his parole. Thom would send him right back inside for the remainder of his sentence. Twenty months. Lord! Worse than the time was what Eva would surely think of him. She would—

Oh, shit!

A cold chill froze him where he stood. The terms of his probation!

He was not supposed to leave Alder County without getting permission from either Thom or the duly elected sheriff. That was the law.

And Overton was in . . . what? Fairfax County? He thought so. Damn sure was not in Alder. That meant he was in violation, right there where he stood. All Thom had to do was to hear about it and Lyle would be on his way back inside.

Oh, Jesus!

He did not know if he could do another twenty.

All right, he could do the time if he had to. But . . . Jesus.

All the pleasure and the excitement of this trip drained right out of him.

Lyle Wilson's shoulders sagged. For the first time since those early days behind stone walls he was once again feeling beaten down to the point of being defeated.

Just when he began to have hope, began to feel that he might have a future, perhaps even a future with a girl as fine as Eva Moore. Now . . . this.

Wilson walked blindly back to the caravan to tell Luis when he should separate the goats that would be sold.

Not that it mattered now. Perhaps he should just let the army buy all the goats, pay off Luis for the work he had put in and wait for Thom to do whatever was required to put him back behind bars.

Jesus!

CHAPTER EIGHTY

Lyle sleepwalked the remainder of his time in Overton. He paid no attention to the amusements in town, and the enticements failed to entice him. His food lacked flavor; beer tasted like water to him and had no more effect. It certainly did nothing to chase his troubles. Those remained with him every waking moment, whether he was eating or drinking or helping Luis with the goats.

On Thursday morning he held the small band of goats that were to be sold. Luis separated the disposable animals from the herd while Elio and the dogs kept the herd together.

The government inspector was a fat, slovenly fellow who introduced himself as a veterinarian—Lyle did not bother to pay attention to the man's name—and descended on them with eight soldiers who were detailed as his assistants. It was obviously a job they were accustomed to by then.

The inspector, a civilian, gave only the most cursory look to each animal he was "inspecting." A glance and a nod and a soldier with a bucket of red paint daubed a smear of crimson onto the goat's hindquarters. Another soldier drove the now-approved animal aside, where the other soldiers held it in a small but growing bunch.

The men shouted and cussed while the goats bleated and tried to escape. Man and beast were covered with the dust of churning hooves. It seemed almost merciful for the dust to clog a man's nostrils because that cut down on his ability to smell the stink of the fresh droppings that seemed to coat the ground underfoot.

But there was nothing wrong with the army's money, Lyle told himself.

He should have been happy, he thought. The government was paying three dollars and a quarter for goats he had paid only two dollars for. That already gave him a profit equal to six months' wages for an ordinary hand. And Luis had done all the work. Come spring Luis would receive half of the increase and Lyle the other half. Plus Lyle would get whatever the mohair brought when the shaggy beasts were shorn, as well as being able to sell the male kids out of his half of the increase. He should have been a happy man. All the more so because of Eva and the way things were going between them.

He shuddered.

Twenty more months. This time he was not so sure he could do it. He might be better off just to turn rabbit and run. Abandon his place. Abandon his livestock. Abandon his name!

It could be done. But . . .

Lord, he wished he knew what to do.

"I'll see you back home the next time you come down for your supplies, Luis."

"*Si*, senor."

"Good-bye, Luis." He climbed wearily into the saddle, took up the mule's lead rope and set off through the crowds and merriment without being touched by any of it.

CHAPTER EIGHTY-ONE

After he returned from the army's purchasing bazaar Lyle Wilson stayed at home for the next eight days, ignoring church and Eva and everything else, until lack of food forced him out into the world again. He was down to flour and a little lard but might have held out even longer except for running out of salt. That was intolerable, so he brought the mare out and hitched her to his wagon.

The horse had not been touched since he got back except for feeding, and she was fresh and feisty.

In a softly crooning voice Lyle cajoled the mare, "Walk, you miserable bitch, walk down now." He sawed at the driving lines and resisted an impulse to let the damn creature run off and break a leg. That would have just about suited his mood. It took a mile or more to get the two of them, Wilson and the horse, calmed and steady.

In town he was relieved to see traffic on Main and business doors open for customers. He had lost track of the days and at the last moment became concerned that it might be a Sunday.

He drew up at the loading dock beside Jim Hanson's store and took his list inside but did not tarry. Conversation was not something he particularly wanted.

"I'll be back in a bit," he told Sarah's mother. "My

wagon is right outside. Thank you, Harriet, I won't be long. G'day now." Lyle touched the brim of his hat and hurried out through the front door.

He turned left on the boardwalk and walked down to the bank.

"H'lo, Dave," he said to the teller. "I need to make a deposit for a change." He fetched the army draft out of his shirt pocket, turned it over and endorsed it before pushing it through the window. "Four hundred sixteen dollars."

"Do you want to deposit all of it?"

"All but the sixteen, I think."

Dave Matthews picked up a selection of forms and rubber stamps and went to work. "By the way," he mused while he worked, "Marshal Thom has been looking for you."

Lyle went cold, yet a bead of sweat began to build on his upper lip.

"I told him I'd tell you next time I saw you," Matthews said.

"Thanks, Dave. I'll look him up when I get a minute. He didn't say what it was about?"

"No. But then he wouldn't, I suppose. Not if it's official business."

Lyle faked a smile. "Could be him and Sarah wanted to invite me to supper or something. Being a bachelor, I don't get much in the way of home cooking."

Matthews chuckled. "The way I hear it, Lyle, you might be changing that bachelor status some time soon."

"Then you'd best tell me about it, because it's sure news to me, Dave." He was serious about that but deliberately let Matthews think he was joking.

Matthews opened his drawer and pulled out a ten-dollar bill plus a half-eagle gold piece and a silver dollar. "Here you go, Lyle. And don't forget your deposit slip." He pushed that through the window too.

"Thanks, Dave. See you."

"Next time."

Lyle stuffed the sixteen dollars into his trousers and hurried back outside. He felt as vulnerable as a bug on a wall. Surely everyone in town could see him. Would know the law wanted him. Would know he was on his way back to prison. Lyle practically ran back to Hanson's store.

"We'll be a while getting this order put together," Harriet told him. "Jim is busy and I don't like to pull orders without him, not since I hurt my back."

"I didn't know about that, Harriet. I'm sorry to hear it."

"Are you in a hurry, Lyle?"

A desperate hurry, dammit. He said none of what he was thinking and hoped none of it showed. "Whenever you can get to it, Harriet."

"Jim will be back after lunch. He's meeting with a salesman. Can you come back in an hour or so?"

"Sure, that will be fine." Again he manufactured a smile. He turned and hurried away.

Lyle had nowhere to go, though. And he did not want to be seen. He did not want to run into Bradley Thom.

He walked at a pace just short of a run out to the edge of town to the Protestant church. The door was closed but he was sure it would not be locked. If no one was inside, that would be so much the better.

Lyle mounted the steps and tried the door. Dammit. Locked. He went around to the side of the building and tried that door. That knob turned under his hand. The latch withdrew.

He opened the door and went inside.

CHAPTER EIGHTY-TWO

Lyle heard a faint sound. He opened his eyes and looked up from his position seated in the second row of pews. Eva was standing in the aisle beside him. She looked startled when her eyes met his.

"I . . . didn't mean to interrupt your prayer," she said.

Lyle said nothing. In point of fact he had not been praying, just sitting there trying not to think about Bradley Thom placing him under arrest again. It was almost certain to happen and in truth he was frightened of it. That, not prayer, had been the focus of his thoughts in the silence of the empty church.

"I knew you were back," Eva said. She slid into the pew beside him and sat, her small body warm next to his. "You didn't come by. Didn't send any sort of word. Have I done something to make you angry?"

She waited as the seconds stretched out to a full minute or more. Finally she spoke again. "I thought you cared something for me."

Lyle's face twisted and a sob escaped through a tightly clenched jaw.

Eva took his arm and lifted it. She slid inside it to snuggle against his chest and sat there is silence, hugging him, waiting for him to regain control of his own emotions. At length she whispered, "Tell me."

And he did. His worries poured out in a rush.

Eva waited and listened, and when Lyle finally was done she pressed herself all the tighter to him. She held onto him and said, "We'll get through this, Lyle. If Bradley does . . . what you think he will . . . if he does that, well, I'll be here when you get back. It is only a year and a half."

Lyle opened his mouth to correct her about the length of his remaining sentence but Eva pressed a fingertip to his lips and said, "I know. Twenty months. That is only barely longer than a year and a half, and if it was another five years, starting all over anew, I would still be here waiting for you. Do you understand that, Lyle? I will be here."

He looked into her eyes for what seemed a long time and then with a sigh pressed his lips to Eva's.

CHAPTER EIGHTY-THREE

"Walk me home?"

"Do you really have to go?" he asked.

Eva nodded. "It's late."

"It hasn't been that long."

"I have to meet with one of the women's committees this afternoon. I have to go home now and change. I only came here to tidy up." She giggled. "I didn't do a very good job of that, did I."

"You did just fine to my mind," Lyle told her. He pulled her to him and kissed her again. Neither of them had left the pew since Eva interrupted his prayers.

She turned her face away. "Seriously, Lyle. I have to go home. Will you walk with me?"

"Don't be silly. Of course I will." Reluctantly he slid out of the pew and stood, extending his hand to help Eva up.

They left the church by the unlocked side door and turned toward the street. Lyle walked rather stiffly at her side. He was surprised when she slipped her hand into his. Right there. In public. He began to beam with pride. It was as good as a declaration of intent. Eva Moore was his girl and she did not mind who knew it. He was not at all sure that his feet touched the earth all the way to the manse. At the gate there Eva lifted herself on tiptoes for a last, quick kiss. "I would invite you in, but . . ."

"No. We'd better not. But I'll see you . . . Could I take you out to supper?"

"Yes, I'd like that."

"Tomorrow night?"

Eva sighed and shook her head. "Prayer meeting tomorrow. How about Thursday?"

"This is Tuesday?"

"Yes, silly. You didn't know?"

Lyle shrugged.

"Thursday. A picnic? Midday? I'll pack a basket," she offered.

"I'll be by to pick you up."

"Yes. Good. I have to run now." But again she paused long enough for a final kiss before turning and passing through the gate and onto the porch, where she stood and watched while Lyle strode away.

He stopped at the street corner and turned back. Eva was still there, standing on the porch watching him. He waved and reluctantly turned away, suddenly fretful that his wagon was blocking the loading dock at Hanson's.

CHAPTER EIGHTY-FOUR

Lyle glanced toward the sky. It was late. Not that he regretted a moment that had been spent with Eva. But it would be dark before he got home. That was not really a concern. Both he and the mare knew the way plenty well by now. He shook out the driving lines and pulled the mare into a tight turnaround in the street to head back toward Main.

"Hold up there, Wilson."

Lyle stopped and swiveled around on the seat. Bradley Thom had come out onto the loading dock. He was scowling. But then Thom appeared to be unhappy most of the time these days.

"What d'you want, Marshal?"

"I came out to your place looking for you a week or so ago. You weren't there."

Lyle waited for the town marshal to continue with what he had to say, but apparently that was all of it. He shrugged. "Sorry I missed your call."

"Don't think I don't know what you're up to."

Lyle snorted. "Ayuh, so you should. What I am up to is raising and selling livestock. Not a damn thing wrong with that. Not even by your reckoning, I should think."

"That all depends on whose livestock it is that you're selling," Thom said.

"You're welcome to check my bills of sale any time, Marshal. My books too, for as long as I'm on probation. I'm well aware of that."

"I may do that too, Wilson." Thom made the simple statement sound like a threat.

Lyle nodded. "Just let me know when you want t' come out so I can make it a point to be there." He turned back around to face forward and shook the mare's lines. The horse started forward at a walk and Wilson quickly put her into a trot. All of a sudden he was anxious to reach the solitary comforts of home.

CHAPTER EIGHTY-FIVE

"Whoa there. Stand and deliver, Wilson, you son of a bitch."

Lyle had been more than half asleep, dozing on the seat of the wagon while the faithful mare pulled him up the hill toward home. It had grown fully dark and the rolling crunch of iron-rimmed wagon wheels on gravel served to lull him to sleep.

His head snapped up now and his eyes came open, but the sky was overcast and admitted no hint of moon or starlight through the layer of cloud. Lyle could not see anything farther than he could reach out and touch.

He blinked and strained to see but could not.

The mare had stopped of her own volition and he guessed there must be someone standing in the road.

"Who are you? What do you want?"

"First thing, Wilson, we want to whip your scrawny ass. Then we're gonna rob you. After that we might kill you."

"Or maybe we won't," another voice put in from a very short distance to the right of the first. Both sounded like they were standing somewhere just ahead of the wagon.

Wilson looked left and right, trying to decide if there might be more than just these two.

"Is that you, Hart? It is, isn't it? And that would make
the other one your asshole buddy Bannerman. Y'
know, while I was in prison I learned what that term
means. But what I'm trying to figure out is which one
of you bastards gets to ride on top when the two of you
are going at it."

He expected to provoke them into losing control.
That would very likely give him the upper hand, as
they would be handicapped by the dark as much as he
was. Instead there was a flurry of cussing and—not at
all what he expected—the bright yellow fan of sudden
light as one of them fired a gun at him.

Lyle cried out and dropped to the floor of the driving box. He hunched down as small as he could make
himself and frantically felt around on the floorboards
in search of the shotgun he had put there to ease Eva's
fears. Had he even remembered to load the damn thing?
Yes. He thought he had.

Out in front of the wagon there were more gunshots,
the explosions sounding oddly dull from in front of
them. The flashes of light were blindingly bright in the
darkness.

He heard more curses. More gunshots.

The wagon lurched, slewing sideways just a little,
and there was the sound of something heavy striking
the earth.

The mare. Damn them, they shot his mare. She was
down.

Lyle found the 12-gauge, wrapped his fist around
the neck of the buttstock and eared both hammers back.
He brought the heavy weapon around.

A rifle or pistol shot lighted up the night directly in
front of the wagon. Lyle leveled the twin tubes of his
gun at the spot where the spear of yellow light had

been and touched off his left barrel. For a brief instant
he could see the mare, down on her knees between the
poles, and the bulk of Willy Bannerman standing immediately in front of her. There was another man's
figure several yards to the right of Bannerman. He assumed that would be Hart but the flash of light from
his gunshot did not last long enough for him to be
sure of that.

Colored lights danced in the darkness that closed in
behind the spray of fire from Lyle's shotgun blast. For
long moments he was blinded. He blinked rapidly, trying to restore as much vision as he could.

He heard a scream of pain and again the sound of a
falling body. Bannerman? Probably. Almost certainly.

"Damn you," a voice shrilled from the spot where
the other man—Hart?—was standing.

Hart fired twice more but the bullets sailed well
above Wilson's head as he crouched on the floorboards
of the immobilized wagon.

"Damn you." This time the voice came from a different direction. Wilson could hear the sound of boots on
gravel, the noises receding up the hillside toward his
right, in the direction of the ridge and, beyond it, town.

Wilson stayed where he was, huddling as low as he
could get inside the wooden sides of the wagon box.
He was trembling, his breath coming fast and short.

If they came back . . .

When they came back . . .

It was a very long time before Lyle Wilson climbed
awkwardly down from the wagon and went to check
on the mare—she was lying dead between the poles—
then started the long walk the rest of the way home.

CHAPTER EIGHTY-SIX

Wilson grunted with effort. The sun was barely off the horizon and he was already running sweat. But that, he thought, was as much from fear and frustration as it was from the effort of trying to remove the dead horse from its harness. The hobbled mule cropped grass contentedly off to the side of the road.

As soon as he had the harness free, Lyle intended to put it onto the mule—Lord, he hoped it would fit—and use it to haul the horse well clear of the road. The carrion eaters, coyotes and magpies and smaller creatures, would soon enough reduce the carcass to bone. But first he had to get the harness free.

A hint of movement caught out of the corner of his eye drew his attention down the road that led toward the blue, sparkling Fox and the highway that ran beside it.

A plume of dust announced that company was on its way. Lyle quickly pulled his jacket on and picked up the shotgun. He broke open the action and checked the loads in the gun. This time, unlike last night, he had extra ammunition in his pockets. He was ready for a fight if that was what the sons of bitches wanted.

Five minutes or so later he could see who was coming. It was an odd collection. Town marshal—and sometimes deputy sheriff—Bradley Thom was leading the pack along with Tom Hart, John Marble and two rough-looking men Wilson did not recognize. In addition to those, the sort Wilson would expect to find in a posse, there were Evan Moore and Leonard Keng. Keng was, for a change, wearing a pistol on his hip.

It took no great leap of the imagination for Lyle to recognize the reason for those last two to be in the bunch. They were there to keep Bradley Thom and his chums from killing Lyle out of hand. They intended, bless them, to see to it that Lyle was not murdered by this posse.

Lyle considered his options. Then he laid his gun in the bed of the immobile wagon. He walked around to the back of the box, dropped the tailgate and sat in the bed to wait for the arrival of his guests.

"Mornin', gents," he said when the posse had drawn rein practically close enough for him to get drooled on by the slobber from their horses' mouths.

"Lyle Wilson," Bradley Thom announced in a voice loud enough to be heard two counties over, "we are here to arrest you for the murder of one William Bannerman, otherwise known as Willy. What say you."

"Son of a bitch died, did he?" Lyle said. He kept his voice low and his hands in plain sight. "Good. Him and that bastard there"—he pointed to Hart—"tried to hold me up and kill me last night some time. I got a shot off at them. If Willy Bannerman died from it, I'm glad. Means he won't be trying to rob me again. Which him and Hart has done before." He stood, forcing Thom's horse to back up. "There's no law in this country to keep a man from defending himself. If Bannerman is dead, it's his own doing."

"I have a witness here who swears that he and Bannerman encountered you on the road last night, that you attacked them without provocation and that you murdered Bannerman in the course of your mayhem. He tells me that he himself barely got away with his life."

"Then he's a lying son of a bitch," Lyle said.

Before Thom could respond the group was disrupted by Leonard Keng's horse, which bolted out of the bunch and circled around, tossing its head and high-stepping its forefeet, until it finally settled near the front of the wagon. Which put the former ranger behind Lyle's back.

Lyle twisted back and forth, trying to keep an eye on Brad Thom and one on Bubba Keng at the same time. His shotgun was under the seat of the wagon, a good three or four paces from where he was now standing. And the scattergun held only two shells anyway. If it came to a fight he was badly outgunned here.

And it was beginning to look more and more like things would come to a fight.

One thing sure. He had done nothing wrong and he did not intend to go back to prison—or worse—on a charge of which he was innocent. He'd done that once before, abiding by a law he had not broken, and now it seemed that only set him up for an even greater betrayal.

Lyle retreated up the length of the wagon, coming closer, ever closer, to the shotgun that lay on the floor beneath the seat.

CHAPTER EIGHTY-SEVEN

"Hold it!" Bubba Keng's voice was sharp. The former Arizona Ranger's tone commanded not only attention but instant compliance. Lyle stopped where he was.

"Take a look at this horse. It was shot straight-on in the forehead, not from behind like it would have been if Wilson did the shooting. Was shot with a bullet from a rifle or a pistol. If you really want to know which, I can dig the slug out and show you." Keng looked around but he had no takers for that offer. "Hart, you claimed Wilson came upon you and started shooting. You never said what you were doing on his ranch."

"We were here on official business," Hart said, spurring his horse ahead. "Brad deputized us t' go up and see could we find the cows Wilson rustled."

"Wilson rustled cows, did he?" Keng asked.

"Damn right he did, and we found 'em. Mayhap that's why he came gunning for us an' shot down poor Willy."

"You say you found the cattle Wilson stole?"

"That's right. Twelve head of Slash S beeves. He's got them stashed in a little cirque high up on that hill behind his place." Hart pointed. "That 'un right there."

"Twelve head of Slash S beef," Keng repeated. "That's what you say he stole?"

"Yes, sir, and I can take you right to them if he ain't

had time to change the brands and run them in with his own bunch yet."

"That's what I heard he was doing last week," Bradley Thom put in. "That's why I came up here looking for him. I wanted to ask him was he rustling cows again and it's why I couldn't find him at home that day. He was off doing his thieving and now we have the proof."

"You say he was going to run those cattle in with his own herd?" Keng asked with a grin.

"That's right. After he changed the brands, he was. That's exactly the way I heard it."

"You don't think those Slash S cows would have stood out amongst Wilson's stock?"

"Not once he changed the brands, no they wouldn't," Thom asserted.

"You knew Wilson was running stock up here, didn't you," Keng said.

"I heard that, yes," the marshal said. "Likely you did too. I think I heard that . . . I don't remember who it was that told me. That was weeks ago anyhow. I knew it would just be a matter of time until Wilson went back to his thieving ways."

"Stole Slash S cows," Keng said.

"Why do you keep saying that," Thom snapped. "Of course he did. And if Tom Hart and Willy Bannerman hadn't found those cows before Wilson changed the brands, they would've been mixed in with his herd before now."

"I can take you up there to them," Hart offered. "I know right where they are."

"Oh, I'm sure you do," Keng said. "And I'm equally sure that you put them there."

"Say now! There's no call to be insulting to the man,"

Thom snapped. "How can you reach a conclusion like that?"

"It's easy enough to do when the two of you talk about Wilson changing the brands on those cows and mixing them in with his own herd," Keng said. The former ranger shifted his attention to one side, where Evan Moore sat perched awkwardly atop a borrowed saddle horse. "Do you know anything about Wilson's livestock, Pastor?"

"Of course I do. We've talked about them."

"Uh-huh. I've talked with him about them too," Keng said.

"What the hell does this have to do with anything?" Thom demanded. "The man is a murderer. He should be strung up."

"That bullet hole in the bay's head proves he is no murderer, and your words show that Hart and Bannerman—probably at your direction—tried to frame Wilson for rustling cattle."

"He did. Tom can take you right to them."

"Oh, I'm sure he can. But Wilson didn't put them there, he and Bannerman did."

"But—"

"Bradley, shut up before you dig yourself into jail. Wilson couldn't add to his herd by stealing cattle. The man is running goats up there, for crying out loud, not cows."

"Marshal Thom," Evan Moore said in a deceptively soft voice, "you have a problem with Lyle. I understand that. A preacher hears things from his congregants, and it would amaze you to know some of the things I've heard about you. If you don't want me to discuss those reports with the sheriff, Marshal, I suggest you leave Lyle alone from now on."

"You can't tell anything you hear in confession," Thom snapped. "I don't know much about you sky pilots but I do know that much anyhow."

"I am not a priest," Evan said. "I'm not bound by any vows like a Catholic priest would be, and I can say whatever I please to whomever I like. That would include the sheriff of this county."

"You wouldn't."

"No. I won't. Unless you force the issue."

"I . . . I don't . . ." Whatever Thom might have said was left unspoken. He yanked on his reins and wheeled his horse away, causing several other mounts in the bunch to bugger and snort.

The Fox Hill town marshal took off down the narrow road toward the public highway with Tom Hart close on his heels. The others hesitated, then drifted along behind those two until only Keng, the preacher and Lyle remained.

"Bannerman is dead, huh?"

Keng nodded.

Lyle shrugged and said, "I can't say that I'm sorry. Can't say that it gives me any pleasure either."

"I don't think our marshal will be bothering you any longer," Keng said.

"I can't say that I understand everything that just happened," Lyle said. "Especially you . . . taking up for a paroled felon . . ."

"You can thank Evan for that. Before I ever met you he told me that you are innocent of the crime you went to prison for."

"But how would he—?"

"Preachers hear things," Evan said. He smiled. "One of the things I've heard lately is that I should brush up on my wedding service."

"That may be well enough for you, Pastor," Keng said, "but right now we need to help Lyle get that harness off the horse and onto the mule. Lyle, lift those poles out of the way, please. Evan, you can help me roll this horse onto its side. All right now. One . . . two . . . three . . ."

Lyle was only dimly aware of what the other two were doing. He was thinking about Eva. Now just where was it, he wondered with a wide grin, that Evan might have heard something about the impending need for a marriage ceremony to be performed?

□ **YES!**

Sign me up for the Leisure Western Book Club and send my FREE BOOKS! If I choose to stay in the club, I will pay only $14.00* each month, a savings of $9.96!

NAME: _____

ADDRESS: _____

TELEPHONE: _____

EMAIL: _____

□ I want to pay by credit card.

□ **VISA**　□ **MasterCard**　□ **DISCOVER**

ACCOUNT #: _____

EXPIRATION DATE: _____

SIGNATURE: _____

Mail this page along with $2.00 shipping and handling to:
Leisure Western Book Club
PO Box 6640
Wayne, PA 19087
Or fax (must include credit card information) to:
610-995-9274
You can also sign up online at **www.dorchesterpub.com**.

*Plus $2.00 for shipping. Offer open to residents of the U.S. and Canada only. Canadian residents please call 1-800-481-9191 for pricing information.
If under 18, a parent or guardian must sign. Terms, prices and conditions subject to change. Subscription subject to acceptance. Dorchester Publishing reserves the right to reject any order or cancel any subscription.